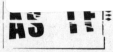

jamie & sooz: love hurts

Sooz on Jamie

Jamie is like this crossbreed of the warmest, funniest, truest friend you could dream to have and the crassest, most insensitive, sex-obsessed juvenile to haunt your darkest nightmare. He and I come out of the same mould. We don't really fit, no one understands our humour except us and we both need people more than we'd like to admit. But there are two huge differences between us. First, he loves Nicki to pieces and I... don't. Second, I am a grown-up.

Jamie on Sooz

Picture the opposite of the girliest girl you can think of and you've got Sooz. Dreadlocks, piercings, tattoos, and a tongue like a razor. Sooz is one scary female. She'll eat you alive if you're not as sharp as she is. Nicki's the total opposite, and she's the one I fancy. Sooz is a really good mate, not like a girl at all. But I can't get close – she won't let me in. She's afraid of what I might find.

Jamie wants Sooz to open up; Sooz wants Jamie to grow up. But we can't always get what we want, as Jamie and Sooz discover. This is their story in their own words.

jamie & sooz
love hurts

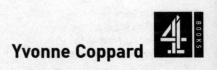

Yvonne Coppard

First published 2002 by Channel 4 Books
an imprint of Pan Macmillan Ltd
Pan Macmillan, 20 New Wharf Road, London N1 9RR
Basingstoke and Oxford
Associated companies throughout the world
www.panmacmillan.com

ISBN 0 7522 6201 7

9 8 7 6 5 4 3 2 1

A CIP catalogue record for this book is available from
the British Library.

Designed by seagulls

Printed and bound by Mackays of Chatham

This book accompanies the television series *As If*,
a Carnival
        films production made in association with
                Columbia TriStar Television for Channel 4.

Director: Brian Grant
Producer: Julian Murphy
Series devised by: Amanda Coe
Executive Producer: Brian Eastman

I know from the look in their eyes that I make them nervous.

Possibly, that last tattoo was a big mistake. I can't even see it without a mirror. It might well look sexy, but who would know? By the time I get a man, my bum will have sagged round my ankles and be so full of wrinkles that the exquisite dragon will look like a grotesque troll.

Usually I'd try a design out in body paint first. But I can't reach the small of my back with a brush. In answer to the obvious question – why not get someone else to do it? – I refer you to the comments above. There is no one in my life I would give a paintbrush and my bare bum to. Not without expecting a considerable reaction of a not entirely positive kind.

It's not that I'm without friends. I'm just without friends of that particular sort. I love hanging out with the gang, but that

SOOZ

doesn't mean I trust them. Would you? In ascending order of trustability, let's consider:

Sasha

Big, bold, beautiful Sasha, our very own Amazon warrior. She can pack a punch to do Lennox Lewis proud, as Rob knows to his cost. Sasha's OK most of the time. But she wouldn't give a toss about my bot, except to try and make sure it didn't look as good as hers. Sasha's into looking good, being the best, staying on top. Poor old Rob struggles to keep up. He thinks he's out of her league — that she's doing him a favour by going out with him.

Truth is, Sasha doesn't appreciate Rob. He deserves someone better. He deserves me.

Nicki

I've got nothing against Nicki, but everyone knows she's a slapper. Sex, shopping and Nicki are Nicki's favourite — actually, only — occupations in life. I didn't realize it was possible for any human being to be totally, utterly and completely shallow until I met Nicki. She is beautiful, in that expensively manufactured way. She has the sort of curvy body film stars would die for. The way she moves, even getting up to go to the bar or hailing a bus, milks every single centimetre of every single curve. She's only seventeen, but I bet she couldn't tell you how many men she's slept with, and she doesn't care. She's a selfish, self-centred cow of a slapper. And she's friends with Sasha — best friends, which makes sense when you see them together. And she's also friends with me. *Not*. We tolerate each other because that's the only way we can keep our other friends. All the same I'd trust her, if I had to, sooner than I'd trust Sasha. One: she's a perfectionist and wouldn't like people to think she'd done a shoddy job, even on my bum. Two: she doesn't hit people, unlike Sasha who's inclined to wallop anyone who annoys her (including Rob).

Rob

Quite simply the most beautiful man I have ever met. He works in the coffee bar, and let me tell you, when he tucks that little order pad into his back pocket and his T-shirt rides up... but he's Sasha's so I won't go there. Not at the moment. That's why I can't ask him to have a go at my body paint. He could probably be trusted, but I wouldn't be able to trust myself.

Alex

Probably my most grown-up friend: he's wise, he's witty, he

understands what I'm saying and he doesn't spend his life obsessing about how to get into some girl's knickers. OK, the main reason for that is he's gay, but he's not always trying to get into some guy's knickers either. Well, only about 80 per cent of the time. And he's quite good at pretending to be straight, because his parents don't know about him. So when I need a pretend boyfriend, he helps out. He never asks me to return the favour, though. This is partly because his mum is always trying to pair him off with a girl so he's never short of offers, and partly because his mum would have a complete eppy if she thought Alex and I were together. She would take to her double divan with matching valance, and never rise again until he swore an undying oath to forsake me in favour of that nice Lydia Whitehouse with the straight teeth and Post Office account. I like Alex's parents, but I know from the look in their eyes that I make them nervous. Alex says it's the nose ring and the shoulder tattoo. They don't have that kind of thing in Almond Avenue.

Alex could be trusted to do a good job – he's quite artistic – but not to keep his mouth shut. My bum would be the hot topic of conversation on campus within the hour.

Jamie

Jamie is like a crossbreed of the warmest, funniest, truest friend you could dream of having and the crassest, most insensitive, sex-obsessed juvenile to haunt your darkest nightmare. He and I come out of the same mould. We don't really fit, no one understands our humour except us and we both need people more than we like to admit. But there are two huge differences between us. First, he loves Nicki to pieces and thinks she's wonderful and I... don't. Second, I am a grown-up. I couldn't bear his naked excitement about getting to see a girl's bum at last. Nor his juvenile jokes and innuendos, which would stretch on for weeks after the event.

Memo to self: next time the tattoo parlour beckons, take a cold shower instead.

A one-woman man

When you've got it, you've got it. And I've got bucket-fuls. Trouble is, although I could have my pick of the available talent, I'm a one-woman man. One woman at a time, I mean. And my one woman of the moment is Nicki, whose one man of the moment is Toby dog-faced Jarvis. I know it's only a matter of time before she sees how much better she can do, but it's hard, waiting.

Nicki. Green eyes, glossy hair, big smile, big boobs... not that I'm the shallow kind of bloke who only looks at a girl's curves. She's cute, kind, funny – like a little Disney creature. There ought to be key rings and cuddly toys and posters and walkie-talkie dolls of her. Life-sized dolls... freeze frame here for a fantasy moment.

jamie

'Jamie, my love, kiss me. I've fancied you for so long, Jamie... now that Toby has fractured his pelvis and broken both arms and legs in that crazy motorbike stunt on Mount Everest, I'm going to need a man who can look after me... Jamie, kiss me. Kiss me all over.'

Phwoah. Not that I wish Toby Jarvis any harm. I'm not keen on pinching other blokes' birds. We need to stick together. Safety in numbers. But if he did happen to meet with an unfortunate accident... Nicki is going to be mine, sooner or later. I just have to wait.

Alex says Nicki is out of my league. Sooz says, 'Yeah. As in her Premier, you Conference.'

Sooz can be such a bitch. Just because no one this side of hell would fancy her, she has to put the boot in for everyone else. She makes me feel weird, Sooz. It shouldn't matter that she dishes it – she does it to everybody, it's water off a duck's proverbial to them. But I don't like it when she gets at me. She can make me feel so... I dunno.

What does Sooz know about anything anyway? She's never even had a bloke so much as look at her. She's scary, is Sooz. Full of tattoos and metal. Not like my soft, warm little kitten, Nicki.

jamie

OK, so how stupid is this?

Best Mates or Bad Memories?

How many real friends have you got, and what does it say about you?

1. What do you look for in a friend?

A. Someone who will stand by you through thick and thin, who you can share anything with.

B. Someone to have a laugh with, no strings attached.

C. Someone who can be useful to you but doesn't take up too much time and energy.

D. You don't look for friends – let them come and find you.

2. What would you say is the difference between a friend and a boyfriend?

A. A friend is for life; a boyfriend is for the moment.

B. A boyfriend is for life; a friend is for the moment.

C. It depends which one you're having sex with.

D. You don't have both, so you can't tell.

3. How many times in the last year have you relied on friends for emotional support?

A. Who knows? You haven't felt the need to keep score.

B. Once or twice, but your friendship is based more on fun than support.

C. About the same number of times you've supported them.

D. What's emotional support?

4. Finally, how many good friends do you have?

A. A circle of 5 or 6 close ones, but loads more as well.

B. More than 4; you can't keep track of everyone.

C. Fewer than 4, but who needs more than that?

D. None at all, come to mention it.

I don't know why I do these quizzes; it's some kind of weird compulsion to find out just how sad I am. I got mostly Ds, of course. All Ds, apart from the one about having no friends. I almost got a D there, too, when I really thought about it, even though there are six of us hanging around together – Me, Alex, Jamie, Nicki, Rob and Sasha. But I can't stand Sasha, and Nicki really gets on my nerves. That leaves Rob, who can hardly be called a friend since he is a love object (what's the real difference between a friend and a boyfriend? The boyfriend is the one you ARE allowed to sleep with). Which leaves Alex and Jamie, whose brains are often away on a visit to their underpants or the latest Lara Croft adventure. Maybe I should have answered D to that one as well.

Mostly Ds

You are a sad git. You need help. Find someone you can talk to and share with, before you die old, lonely and miserable.

Cheers.

Rob. Robbie. Robert. Roberto... there's no ugly way to say that name. If I had a best friend, it would be him. He is probably the most beautiful man I know – inside, out, back to front, all the way round best man I've ever seen. And I can't get him out of my head. They would be wetting themselves, the others, if they knew how I really feel about Rob. Sooz, the spitting cat-woman, fiend from hell, give her a wink and she'll have your eyes out, falling for Mr Gentle. Yeah, right. In her dreams.

So how come I'm the bitch from hell, and Sasha the Slasher and her sidekick Nicki No-knicks are the Princesses Goody-Two Shoes? You tell me.

'I've given jumpers to Oxfam with better personalities...'

Sooz again, moaning about Nicki. Sometimes I wonder about Sooz, like maybe she has a little crush on me. Or she can't bear to see proper women making it. I dunno. Who cares? Newsflash just came through: TOBY JARVIS IS HISTORY! I'm going to have Nicki all to myself!

Jamie Collier, man of action, needs no second telling when it comes to an opportunity. Of course, Nicki's going to be a bit down. It wouldn't be right to jump on her too fast. Toby's touch is still warm on her velvet skin – lovely use of words there, perhaps I should be a writer. But I'm a lot more subtle than that. Start small, work your way up... so to speak.

jamie

Nicki is meeting me on Saturday night at the Purple Parrot. Everyone else is going to be at the Spread Eagle. With masterly cunning I manipulated the situation to my advantage. God, I should give lessons. Nicki will wonder what's going on when she turns up and there's only me. But I only need a couple of minutes alone with her, and it will all be fine. I can't believe it – Nicki and me are going to get it on at last. I won't let her down; I'll be everything she wanted and more.

Toby Jarvis – who he?

jamie

It *is* eye-catching, isn't it? It didn't work, though. Nothing ever seems to work for me. All I wanted was a few men with tattoos to come up to my room, strip off and let me photograph them.

Do get your mind out of the gutter. Purely in the interests of art. If anything else had happened, it wouldn't be because I'd planned it. But not a single bloke stepped up.

That was humiliating enough. But then Jamie stuck the knife in. It started off as a bit of a joke. Jamie said he was thinking of having a tattoo done, and I could use him in my project. We were kidding around about what kind of tattoo he would go for. We had some wild ideas, just as a laugh. We all know Jamie wouldn't go near a needle.

Then it somehow wasn't funny any more. Jamie said I'd be gagging for his tattoo, I said only in my saddest of sad dreams. He said no one would answer my ad. I said it was early days. Then suddenly:

'None of the blokes I know would go near you for a bet.'

He just said it, right out. Like it was a statement of fact, like everyone knew and he was just stating the obvious. It hurt so much, and so fast, that I almost fell down. And while I was still reeling from that, he had another pop:

'No offence. But there's nothing sexy about being the bitch from hell, is there?'

I had to hurt him back, and fast.

'Yeah, well, at least people don't ask me to leave them alone in the street!'

Jamie looked like a little boy who'd been reminded there's no Father Christmas. He made a pass at Nicki a couple of days ago and she told him where to get off. Then when he met up with her by accident in the street she told him to shove off and stop following her. If you want a true selfish bitch from hell, look no further. Fair enough, she doesn't fancy him, but does she have to humiliate him? Being Nicki, yes.

SOOZ

And I rubbed his nose in it. I don't know why I do that: hurt people. It's not like Jamie is even an equal match. He never means to hurt anyone; he's just a little boy. He's got no idea of the ways of the big bad world, and you can swat him like a fly. It's mean to try and hurt people like Jamie. Knowing that doesn't stop me, though.

I feel dirty. My head is banging and my insides feel like a mess of metal and barbed wire. I hate myself. I always hate myself. But I can't change. What you see is what you get. And what you see is, apparently, so unattractive that blokes are scared to come near me and girls don't want to be associated with me.

I think what Jamie said hurt more than anything because he's the one I usually rely on to make me feel better when I'm down. He hasn't got a mean bone in his entire scrawny little body. He comes out with some real crap sometimes, but he always tries to make things better and he never, ever tries to hurt anyone. Being with Jamie is like being with a basket of golden-haired puppies.

Not that I'd ever tell him that. But just because I can't share my deepest feelings or do the giggly girlie thing, doesn't mean I'm the bitch from hell. Does it?

I never realized how deep a person I am.

A lesser man would be feeling a tad defeated at this moment. He would be looking for a hole to crawl into and wishing he could stay there for a long time.

My cunning plan to get Nicki alone at the Purple Parrot went pear-shaped when Rob showed up. Nicki had decided to try and get him back with Sasha, so she asked him along. Of course, there was no Sasha. She was with the others at the Spread Eagle, because that's where she thought Nicki would be... my brain's beginning to hurt.

So we had a gooseberry pie situation. But there again, her being so kind and caring is one of the things I love about Nicki, so it wouldn't be right to complain.

I was making the best of it, being a trooper. I even

jamie

managed to turn the situation to my advantage. We were almost in a clinch. I certainly had a good view down her cleavage. I was expressing concern for her getting sucked into other people's problems. Girls really go for that caring stuff, don't they? Nicki can get sucked into my problems any time she likes, I thought – and I didn't even say it out loud. That's how well I was doing.

The moment came. She was in my arms... well, my arms were in that general direction. I moved in for a gentle kiss on those soft, full lips. Heaven was a hair's breadth away (see how poetical she makes me?)...

'God! I don't fancy you, alright?'

She pushed me off. She looked shell-shocked. Did I misread the signals?

Or is she only just waking up to the possibilities of how good we could be together?

I'll tell you something though, I reckon I'd be better off with an older woman, someone who knows her own mind. I've been messed about too often by girls who are too young to know what they want. Somewhere there's a mature, full-blooded, sexy woman who's just waiting for me to come along. And I'm gonna find her.

I never realized how deep a person I am, and how

jamie

much I've matured over the last couple of years. Look how calm and sensitive I was when Rob dropped that bombshell about him and Sasha. They've never slept together. Never. Not once. No jiggy-jiggy whatsoever. How many blokes could have heard that from a best mate without making a racket? But not me. I listened, I was supportive.

I ought to try and pass on my mind for posterity. A book or something. Yeah, a book. *Jamie Collier, Man of Destiny...* or maybe something simpler. *Jamie on Life, Love and...* I'll have to think of something else beginning with 'L' for that last bit, but otherwise it's a good title.

Meanwhile, I'd better hope that Sasha doesn't find out it was me who told Nicki about her and Rob not doing it, or I'll be missing a vital part of my anatomy when I step up to collect the world book prize.

jamie

He was here, in my room, stripping off.

Those who say I don't do girlie should have seen me last night. I girlied for England – Europe, even. I was more girlie than Barbie will ever be. I had a scary glimpse into what life must be like for Nicki, doing this kind of crap every day. I exfoliated, I buffed, I moisturized. I bought an entire new make-up kit. It cost me a fortune.

'A new look?' The woman at the market stall beamed at me with that we-are-all-girls-together expression. It made me want to slap her.

'Very wise,' she mouthed, with a broad wink. 'Keep him guessing, eh? Different woman every time he comes home, that's the way to keep him.'

sooz

'As a matter of fact,' I said, not being able to help myself, 'this stuff is for my mum. Both my boyfriends are happy with the bondage and rubber at the moment.'

The beam wavered, the plucked eyebrows disappeared under the impossible hair (I bet the package said chestnut, but it was actually maroon. Yes, maroon – as seen in school uniforms, this woman's head, and nowhere else on earth). She didn't know what to say. I passed on the free make-up lesson advertised just above her head, and retreated with my cram-full carrier.

Back home I studied my face in the mirror, plonked concealer on every possible sign of zit, and highlighted my brow bones. I even splodged perfume on my cleavage, or what in my case passes for cleavage. More Smartie than dumpling, as Jamie would say. The sexy perfume came courtesy of Nicki. Very nice. Some posh French designer stuff. The ultimate sign of a girl with more money than sense. Or taste. Or morals. Or anything between the ears except a slapper's radar for male hormone and a tight bum.

I bet that's got you wondering. Nicki, lending Sooz her best perfume? How can this be? Well, she was visited by the ghost of nightclubs past who warned Nicki to mend her selfish ways or be doomed. She saw the light, decided to embrace

Sooz as a sister, and now shares everything she has with the poor, and Sooz.

No? All right, I borrowed it. Down at the café, while she was flirting and wiggling her chassis in front of another poor sucker, I just found my hand wandering into her Gucci leather and pulling out some smelly.

So I pruned and preened and thieved – for what? For one night with Rob. Not even a whole night, just a couple of hours really. But worth it? Oh yes.

I couldn't believe it when he said he'd come round and let me photograph his tattoo.

'You don't have to,' I said, and I could have kicked myself. I sounded about thirteen.

'No, I want to,' he said.

And he came. He was here, in my room, stripping off. It was hard to stop my hands shaking while I was taking the pictures. We talked, really talked, without all the jibing and mickey-taking that goes on when we're all together in a group. When he said he'd like me to paint his back I had to remind myself to start breathing. I could have suffocated, I was so excited and nervous and... well, you can imagine, finally getting to touch someone you've dreamed about for months. Imagine how that feels.

SOOZ

Rob – Rob! – was lying on MY bed, and letting me smooth and stroke and caress his back while I got it ready for painting. And I didn't think about how he was only doing it to make Sasha jealous, or about how he could never really belong to me. Why would a guy like him even consider someone like me? All I thought about was what it was like to have him all to myself, without any interruptions. I thought about where it could lead, now he and Sasha have had a row. No one could accuse me of stealing him. Whatever happened, this moment could never be spoiled.

Cue Jamie. Just when I was beginning to think Rob and I might start to make a bit of progress, the phone rang. Jamie.

'In a bra size, is a double D – like – really big?'

After you've known Jamie a while, you know better than to ask.

I said, 'Much too big for you, Jamie. I'd say you're a 34A, tops,' and chucked the phone down.

You know the guy who can never take a hint? He looks like Mr Super-Sensitive next to Jamie. He called again.

'Are we talking Pamela Anderson or Mighty Jugs Jenkins? All I want to know.'

With Jamie, you may as well give in. He never, ever goes away.

SOOZ

'Ample, yet not deformed,' I said.

That seemed to satisfy him. But just then, Rob asked me something, and Jamie heard his voice.

'What are you doing with Rob?'

All at once there was a chance to be a woman of mystery who had a man who actually fancied her and who was in her room doing mysterious things. Not Sooz, the bitch from hell who terrifies blokes and can't get a man to go near her even for a bet, but Sooz the sex kitten with the most gorgeous man in the world doing her bidding.

So I said, 'Wouldn't you like to know?' and put the phone down.

I knew it would be all round the campus – Jamie would tell Alex, that would be enough – and it felt good. For a moment I even thought it might not be such a fantasy, Rob and me. After all, Sasha might dump him, if she believed the talk. And once he knew what a bitch Sasha was... I was there, available; we were getting on really well...

I told Rob who it was, on the phone, and I told him Jamie was bound to gossip.

Rob smiled. 'Don't be daft. Not even Jamie would believe that!'

Then he said, 'I had a good time today.'

SOOZ

'Me too,' I said.

Don't blow it, Sooz, I thought. Don't go all hard and prickly to cover for being nervous. Go for it. I even moved closer, started to lean forward to kiss him. I was so ready to tell him exactly how I feel.

'We could talk, without all that other stuff getting in the way... 'cos it would have been weird, with a girl,' he said.

Bubble burst. Prickle alert. Defend yourself, Sooz.

'I am a girl,' I said.

'I mean, like, a real girl – like one I fancy and stuff.'

I just about held it together while I got him out of the room. Said goodbye, reminded him to wash the make-up off his back, saw him off with a cheery wave.

'See ya!' I would have died rather than shown how cut-up I was.

But I am a real girl. I am.

Alex,
Nipped round to borrow your 'Crapheads' T-shirt. You were out but your mum said it would be OK.

I'll give it back tomorrow night. Ta, mate.

It's gonna be a hot night, and your T will be a part of it. Be proud!
(Her name's Ellie and she's worth the T, man.)

Jamie

Rob,
I figured you wouldn't need your cargoes, since they were under my bed. So I borrowed them — hot, hot date with one red-headed and passionate Ellie. Don't worry, I'll wash them before I give them back — if I'm wearing them long enough to be worth it...

See ya later,
Jamie

jamie

Sooz,

Yeah, all right — you're forgiven for being A1 evil bitch material yesterday but it's payback time. Can you ring me when you get in? I need help. Hot tottie lined up for tonight, expecting great stuff. Want sexiest tattoo possible for when she rips shirt off. Needs to be extra sexy and non-smudge. You're the man for the job! Call soon!

Love,
    Jamie

Hi Ellie,

Just dropped by to see if you wanted to have that drink we agreed to go for some time. Sorry again about crashing into you. Hope you got all your stuff back in your art folder. If you're back before about 9 or 10 or 11, I'll see you in the Purple Parrot and buy you a drink to make up for it, yeah? I'll be there most of the night, probably.

Jamie

Dear Ellie,

Sorry I missed you in the Purple Parrot. Another time, eh? Call me.

Jamie

Sorry.
Didn't give you my phone number. 772356.
Call me.

Jamie

jamie

This is my first time.
Be gentle.

> HELLO. IS ANYBODY OUT THERE?

> *YES. I'M MARIE.*

> Hi, this is Yvette.

> WOW! COOL NAMES. I'M JAMIE. I FOUND YOU BY ACCIDENT REALLY. I HAVE THIS THING ABOUT TYPING IN RANDOM WORDS ON THE SEARCH ENGINE AND SEEING WHAT I GET. I TYPED IN RELIEF AND PERSONAL.

> *AND YOU GOT US.*

> Destiny, maybe?

> YEAH, DESTINY. I'M NOT SURE HOW IT ALL WORKS. DO I START, OR DO YOU?

> *WHY DON'T YOU TELL US A BIT ABOUT YOURSELF, JAMIE?*

> RIGHT. I'M A YOUNG EXECUTIVE IN A STOCKBROKER COMPANY. TALL, ATHLETIC – PLAY SQUASH EVERY

WEDNESDAY. BUT WHAT WITH ALL THE HIGH-POWERED EXEC MEETINGS AND JETTING OFF TO NEW YORK EVERY FIVE MINUTES, I DON'T SEEM TO HAVE TIME TO CULTIVATE PROPER RELATIONSHIPS.

> You're lonely, Jamie?

> YES. VERY LONELY. I'M LOOKING OUT NOW ACROSS THE ROOFTOPS OF CANARY WHARF AND WONDERING WHAT IT'S ALL FOR. I GET VERY FRUSTRATED AND PENT UP – THAT'S WHY I FOUND YOUR ADVERT SO INTERESTING. '*LET THE FEMALE FORCES BRING YOU PERSONAL RELIEF ACROSS THE NET*'. NICE SALES PITCH.

> *YVETTE AND I CAN HELP YOU, JAMIE. YOU SOUND VERY TENSE. RELAX, LET YOUR MIND CLEAR, FEEL YOUR BODY START TO LET GO.*

> Try to feel us entering your mind. Feel our breath upon the back of your neck. And when you are totally receptive, we will start our encounter.

> WHAT, BOTH OF YOU AT ONCE?

> We try always to work in pairs; two women together offer so much more energy.

> COOL. THIS IS MY FIRST TIME. BE GENTLE.

> Are you ready?

> YOU BET. DO YOUR STUFF.

jamie

> *WE CALL UPON THE FORCES OF MOTHER EARTH, THE PROVIDER, TO RID THIS MAN OF THE EVIL TOXINS THAT FLOOD AND CORRUPT HIS BODY. UNSEX HIM HERE, AND MAKE THE FEMININE IN HIM RISE TO THE SURFACE, BLOTTING OUT ALL BASE DESIRES.*

> Let the old Adam, cast out from the garden of Eden on a testosterone tide, writhe in base agony and be born anew, embracing only the feminine and sub-jecting himself utterly unto Her.

> ACTUALLY I'M NOT BIG ON THE DOMINATRIX STUFF. NOT TO START WITH. I'D RATHER KEEP MY MASCULINI-TY. AND I'M GETTING A BIT TOO PENT UP TO WAIT. THE THOUGHT OF YOUR BREATH ON MY NECK DID THE TRICK ALREADY. COULD WE GET TO THE MORE EXPLICIT BIT, DO YOU THINK?

> *WHAT DO YOU MEAN? WHAT EXPLICIT BIT?*

> THE RELIEF. 'CALLING ALL MEN: DO YOU NEED URGENT RELIEF FROM THE PRESSURES OF YOUR MASCULINITY? CALL THE FEMALE FORCES NOW FOR SALVATION AND RESCUE.' THAT'S THE BIT I WAS AFTER.

> Hang on – do you think we're some kind of sexual chatline?

> NOT EXACTLY. I THINK. I DON'T KNOW. WHAT ARE YOU?

jamie

> *WE ARE THE DAUGHTERS OF EVE, YOU SICK MAN. A RELIGIOUS CHARITY OFFERING ESCAPE FROM MALE PERVERSION.*

> We reach out to men who are trying to escape their masculinity, men who realize that every man is destined to be a twisted pervert, men who want to restore the harmonious balance Mother Nature intended.

> SORRY. MY MISTAKE. I THINK I GOT THE WRONG END OF THE STICK.

> *YOU CERTAINLY DID, YOU DISGUSTING LITTLE PERV. GET OUT OF OUR CHAT ROOM.*

> We'll pray for you.

> THANKS. SORRY. DIDN'T MEAN ANY OFFENCE. YOU DON'T HAPPEN TO KNOW WHAT I'D NEED TO TYPE IN FOR THE OTHER KIND OF RELIEF DO YOU?

> HELLO? IS ANYBODY THERE?

jamie

...dithering like a proper little girlie

I think – can't be sure, not very good at this kind of thing – but I *think* I just had one of those girlie mag moments. Actually, I think I just had *two* moments. That would be weird enough. But one of them was with *Jamie*.

Sorry, going too fast. I'll go back to the party, the other night. All the usual suspects were there. Serge (gorgeous, sexy, French) came on to me. He doesn't speak English, but believe me he didn't need words. Stroking my arm, looking into my eyes... the message was loud and clear.

Of course, being Sooz the Stupid, I mucked it up. I was so shocked, I ran away to Alex.

'The French guy just made a move on me,' I said.

'What are you doing here, then?' said Alex. You can rely on Al to get straight to the point.

Serge was still looking.

What *was* I doing? I can't remember how long it's been since a guy even looked at me, never mind with *that* kind of look. And I can't have Rob, so why was I dithering? Time to move on.

Everyone thinks I'm a hard cow, but really I'm so scrunched up and unconfident inside that I have to get advice from someone before I can let a man near me. I always assume someone's doing it for a laugh, or a bet, or to make someone jealous (like Rob, that time in my room).

I dithered. Hard cow Sooz stood dithering like a proper little girlie for all of thirty seconds before trying to get back to Serge. That's all the time it took for Her to move in and steal my one pathetic little chance.

She's so good at it. The slinky walk, the sudden eye contact, the slow, sexy smile. A hand brushes across her face, moves a strand of hair. She looks away, looks back, smiles. Dead easy.

I won't go into the humiliating details of that moment before I'd realized that Serge was looking at her, not me. Let's just say I presented myself as someone obviously on offer, and his glance barely even flicked over me before he brushed past me to get to her. Two minutes later they were dancing like a well-oiled sex machine. You didn't have to be a clairvoyant to see them ten minutes into the future, ripping the clothes off each other.

Alex, bless him, tried to cheer me up, but it was too much. Suddenly, I saw Nicki looking at me, with that knowing little smile. She knew. She knew I'd had a chance with Serge and she, who can have any man she wants, chose to move in on mine.

I headed for the door. I had to get away. I knew I was going to cry. What would that do for the hard girl image? I wanted to get to a very dark place, curl up, and sob my heart out. But I couldn't get the door open. I released some adrenalin by giving it a good kicking.

Rob came up.

'You going?'

Please, I thought, please don't be nice to me.

'Open the door, please?' I said.

'Well, you're not going home on your own, are you?'

My voice sounded strangled, with all the tears that were choking me.

'Just can you open the door for me, please, Rob.'

'OK.'

He did it. I grabbed my coat off the banister, and left.

SOOZ

He followed me into the street, and said he wanted to walk me home.

'Not tailing Sasha tonight?' I said.

'No, and never again.'

'Yeah, we've all heard that one before, Rob.'

'No, I mean it.' He sounded really insistent. I thought my insides were already about as tangled as they were going to get, but another spring suddenly went. Could he possibly mean what he was saying?

'We should go out for a drink sometime –'

I looked around to see if he was saying it to make Sasha jealous, but we were alone. He meant it. He actually wanted to meet up for a drink. With me.

Of course, I can't call it a date. Not a proper one. He could see I was upset, he just felt sorry for me. But it's a start, isn't it?

Anyway, the really weird thing is, the next day I was talking to Jamie and suddenly the conversation went serious. Don't ask me how. One minute we were doing our usual comedy pair routine – him halfwit, me wasp-woman – and the next he's saying I never tell him anything.

'That's 'cos there's nothing to tell, Jamie,' I said.

'I tell you everything about my love life.' He was looking

sort of earnest and, blow me, serious! I tried to get the jokey Jamie back.

'Real and imagined' I laughed. But he was like a dog with a bone.

'So, I'm still straight with you. Why can't you even admit you liked that, er, Serge or whatever his name was?'

'Because I didn't,' I lied.

'Who then? You must fancy someone.'

'Well, I don't.' He was coming too close. My heart started thumping.

Then he said, quite seriously, 'You're either lying or you're more of a block of ice than I thought.'

That hurt.

'And if you're lying,' he went on, 'cheers, 'cos I thought we were supposed to be best mates.'

I knew he was right. He's a big kid and he drives me mad sometimes, maybe even most of the time. But Jamie and me, we're special in a weird, warped kind of way. A pair of bookends, we are. And I never, ever open up to him. No wonder he thinks I'm like ice. I thought how much I didn't want to be that way, how good it would be to have someone to talk to. I knew that if I was ever going to trust anybody in this life, it would be Jamie. So, quite unexpectedly, it slipped out.

'Rob,' I said – quick, and low, in a rush. Mammoth effort.

And Jamie didn't hear me.

'What?'

'Forget it,' I said.

'Sooz.'

'Nothing.'

'Come on!' He looked into my eyes and I saw that he wasn't just after gossip; he really cared about me. I felt like crying. I've felt like that a lot, lately. It must be hormones or something. 'The adolescent hormonal storm' as our old Health Education teacher would have it.

'Rob,' I said. 'Rob.'

Clear as a bell, no mistake.

Jamie sat, stunned. Finally, he said, 'He's a sound bloke.'

'I know,' I said.

He looked at me, hesitated, and then said, 'Of course the whole Sasha thing—'

As if I needed reminding.

'I KNOW!' I snapped.

He looked hurt. I smiled to show him I didn't mean it.

We sat there, on the bench, both trying to think of something to say. We were having a grown-up conversation, me and Jamie, and it was new territory. I don't think either of us knew what to do next. It was awkward.

'I didn't ditch Gabi,' Jamie said suddenly. 'She ditched me. I really liked her. Just too young, too stupid. For anyone.'

I knew he was trying to show me he understands what it's like to want someone who doesn't want you. I'd been teasing him about Gabi. I never realized how serious it had been for him. All that time, taking my jokes, shrugging his shoulders, telling me he didn't care and he'd had to ditch her because she was too needy.

I was overwhelmed. I realized that a lot of Jamie is an act, just like a lot of me is an act. We're both softer than we look; we both hurt easily and don't know how to show it. I felt closer to Jamie then than I've ever felt to anyone, but I couldn't think of a single thing to say.

So I reverted to the Old Sooz fallback position.

'Come on,' I said. 'I'll buy you a bag of chips.'

We were back to our old selves. Almost. But something happened on that park bench that I don't understand. I still want Rob; I don't fancy Jamie any more than I fancy next-door's dog. But there's something extra between us now, a kind of bond that's more than a couple of kids having a laugh.

...the most incredible experience of my whole life.

Gabi.

Gabi and me were special.

Why can't I write about it? I try to. I start a new line, hoping it will help. But I can't write a word. I wanted to write poems. But my poems are crap. I never show them to anyone. People just laugh. It didn't matter to me that Gabi was a bit older. A lot older, then. With a kid. And a husband. With her, *I* was older. I look at my life now, now that she's gone, and it looks like a little kid's life. It's empty and it doesn't mean anything.

It's been a joke from start to finish as far as all my mates are concerned. Jamie's fantasy bird, picked up on the Internet. Jamie the cybersex freak. I bet they spend most of their lives trying to get half of what me and

jamie

Gabi had. You have no idea, unless you've done it, how powerful cybersex attraction can be. Or how dangerous.

'Run along, Jamie, Mummy's here,' Sooz said once, when Gabi came by.

It was all such a laugh. Wouldn't you just know it would be Jamie Clown-Collier who went and got himself tangled up with an older woman, trying to get inside her knickers by computer?

'Go on, Jamie, tell us all about it. Type in "get 'em off"and see if we can hear her bra twang across the air waves... can you see her red lacy cyber-thong, Jamie?'

Yeah, funny.

That first time we met, Gabi and me, it was magic. I started off badly, like a kindergarten kid talking to Santa. We met at Holland Park station. There'd been loadsa jokes about what Jamie's older bit of stuff would look like.

'So, how're you going to recognize her?' Louise asked.

Sooz, quick off the draw as ever, said, 'She'll be the one with the two heads...'

'And a T-shirt – "I love Chernobyl"' said Alex.

Ho bloody ho. Couldn't they see how nervous I was?

'Serve him right if she's some poor geri of about eighty,' said Sooz.

jamie

'Wham bam thank you gran,' said Alex.

'A bit of how's your mother,' Sasha laughed.

Then Louise said, 'Erm, what if it *is* his mother?'

I hung around for a couple more jibes about it probably being a man etc., etc., etc., and then got the hell out of there.

Gabi wasn't a man, or a geri, or my mum. She was simply the most beautiful, tender, graceful, lovely woman I have ever met. As soon as I clapped eyes on her, I started gabbling on about buses and trains, and which number goes where, and which ones have the best disabled facilities. God, I just quake when I remember what a dill I was in those first few minutes. Alex and Sooz would have wiped the floor with me. But Gabi understood. She knew how nervous I was. Maybe she felt the same. She calmed me down, gave me a second chance.

'So how old are you?' she asked.

'Er, well, I'm not quite twenty-five.'

'I can see that.'

'If you want the truth I'm twelve,' I said, and she laughed. She had a lovely laugh.

After half an hour it was like we'd been together for years. We packed a lifetime into one night. Drinks, a club, salsa. Walking, talking...

jamie

Sex? No.

Not sex. Lovemaking. Now I know why they call it that. It was the most incredible experience of my whole life. Outside, under the stars, with all the lights of London twinkling across the river like a little orchestra of gypsy musicians. Maybe I can write poetry.

I tried to tell the others about Gabi. I wanted to share it. But it was all a big joke to them. So I told Gabi everything instead. All that love was just bursting out. So I told her. On the Net.

I WANT YOU.

I NEED YOU.

I WANT TO DOWNLOAD MY LOVE FOR YOU.

She didn't type anything back. But it didn't matter. I knew she would tell me everything I wanted to hear when we met. We were way past cybersex now.

But she dumped me, didn't she? Just like that. I gave her every last little tiny scrap of everything I am and will ever feel on that first night together. And Gabi? For her, I found out, 'It was a bit of a laugh.'

'You have to have these feelings for somebody your

jamie

own age. Jamie... I'm twenty-nine.... You can't give me what I want... you're just a kid.'

That was the bottom line, for her. I was just a kid.

I told Sooz and the others I had dumped Gabi, because she was too needy. But I almost told Sooz the truth. God knows why. Sooz, more than anyone, can slice open a wound and rub salt in it. She's got a tongue like a razor, and she enjoys making mincemeat out of people who aren't as good with words as she is. Still, I almost told her.

'I was thinking, Sooz,' I said. 'You were right all along. I went into this thinking about sex. I never thought about love, or that maybe anyone would get hurt. But I should have done.'

I suppose I wanted to talk. I was hoping that Sooz would say something kind, for once, and give me a chance. But she looked at me as if I was weird, and thumped my arm. So I didn't tell her what Gabi had said.

'She was really upset when I dumped her,' I said. Then I smiled, and thumped Sooz back.

The jokes went on, about Gabi and me, but I pretended I didn't care and started looking around. Plenty more fish in the sea, a good-looking guy like me.

Then Sooz had a bad night. Some French creep called

jamie

Serge made a move on her at a party. I think she fancied him, but Nicki got there first. Well, no contest. What red-blooded male is going to muscle past a goddess to curl up with a little Sooz-creature? Right.

Usually Sooz spits and snarls a bit, finds a cool way to settle the score and then moves on. But this time it really seemed to get to her. She looked smaller, caved in, like a light had gone out somewhere. I wanted to help, but she wouldn't let me.

That's when we had this strange thing on the bench near college. I wanted to know what was up. I was trying to get her to talk. We weren't making much progress. Especially when Nicki showed up.

Last time I'd seen Nicki, she was making a collection to help Louise pay a stallholder for the criminal damage she caused to his priceless fake zebra skins. Nicki had told her they were real, so Louise sabotaged them with a bottle of ketchup, on the spot. Poor old Louise never could resist a chance to fight injustice. And she's a bit thick, which doesn't help. Anyway, I gave Nicki what I had (Sooz said it was all Nicki's fault in the first place, so she should be the one paying), and I thought it was only polite to catch up on progress.

'How's the collection going?' I asked.

jamie

'It isn't,' Nicki said, and flounced off. It was, I have to say, a very adorable and flirty flounce.

Sooz, naturally, wasn't sympathetic.

'She's really got that wounded doe act down to a T, hasn't she?'

'You're just bugged about that French guy,' I said.

'I am so not.'

'You can't handle the fact that she can have anyone she wants and you can't,' I said.

It was meant to be just our normal routine. She gets at me, I get at her. Nothing personal. It's our form of exercise, Sooz's and mine. Like working out together, but without the sweat. But this time, there was something about the look on her little sharp face that made things take a different turn, somehow.

'Yeah, well, who is there to want?' she said. She was trying to be her usual couldn't-give-a-toss self, but I could see something there. I've got radar when it comes to Sooz.

'You tell me,' I said.

She wouldn't, of course, but you could see there was something to tell. So I went at it like a dog with a bone – I didn't let go. And I made her tell me what was getting her down.

jamie

Rob. She fancies Rob. As in, Sasha's Rob.

What was I supposed to say? I mean, do you think she's stupid enough to fall for, 'Tell you what Sooz, you're so much more gorgeous than Sasha, it's only a matter of time...' 'Course not.

I didn't have the faintest what to say. I felt all muddled up inside. She was hurting like I was hurting. Both of us were longing for someone we couldn't have. Only of course she didn't know about Gabi and me.

So I told her. Gabi dumped me, I said, I didn't dump her. Sooz didn't look as gobsmacked as I thought she would, but she understood what I was saying. This was a time to stick together, help each other out. And neither of us was going to make a cheap shot out of it.

Any other woman would have turned it into a telly soap episode, with lots of heart-to-heart talking and stuff. We would have been in each other's arms, sharing secrets and stroking each other. It would probably have led to a snog, maybe a shag. That seems to happen when people get upset.

I could have handled that. But it's never been Sooz's way to do what the girlies do.

'Come on,' she said. 'I'll buy you a bag of chips.'

jamie

She'll never take a glass of sherry of an evening again.

Jamie is so easy to wind up, you almost feel bad doing it. Almost. He's still not speaking to Alex and me. Claims he was 'humiliated'. But how do you humiliate someone like Jamie? He's so up for everything, so insensitive to innuendo. He's completely unhumiliate-able.

He blew into the café, pinched my coffee with a breezy smile and wanted, as usual, to be an instant part of whatever was going down. At that moment, what was going down was a plan by Sasha-Slasher to get Rob to come back to her. She and Nicki No-knicks were whispering away in a corner thinking no one could hear them. But me and Al were earwigging. Big Saturday night seduction was being planned in Sasha's flat while her mum was off for the weekend. Rob was supposed to be having a drink with *me* on Saturday. I know Sasha didn't know that, but I still felt like smacking that smug smile off her face. She thinks she can just reel him in whenever she feels like making a bit of an effort. The sickening thing is, she may be right. In any case, what could I do about it? Show up on the doorstep and launch into a 'get your hands off my man' scene? Not my style. Arsenic in the spritzer, that's more me.

Then along comes Jamie. Bless.

'What are those two up to?' he said, straight away. Sasha and Nicki have an unmistakable look about them when they're in plotting mode.

'They're planning,' said Alex.

'Girlies,' I said.

'Yeah, what's that then?' Jamie's face was all a-quiver in anticipation of gossip.

'Ah, don't wanna get involved,' I said, but I know Jamie. He wasn't going to accept that.

'Oh really?' He was like a fish, flirting with the line, ready to swallow the hook.

The great thing about Alex is, he's on my wavelength. Just one look passed between us, and the wind-up was on.

'Tell us,' urged Jamie.

Alex squirmed in his seat, and looked uncomfortable. I tried not to laugh.

'Look mate,' said Alex, 'it's not really for us to say.'

'Oh come on, what? Is it illegal or something?'

His little face was aglow with expectation. He was even feeding us ideas for how to keep him wriggling. We couldn't disappoint him, could we?

Alex looked at me again. 'Well, it could be,' he said. 'If it all goes according to plan...'

My brain went into overdrive, trying to think ahead, plan how to keep it going. But Jamie fed us again.

'Are we talking about a party?'

Alex didn't answer and neither did I. We were considering how that idea might run. But Jamie took the pause to mean 'yes'.

'We are! Oh, right, thanks guys, thanks for telling me about it.' He looked really upset, thinking he'd been left out.

'Come on mate,' I said, 'you're overreacting.'

Al tried to be comforting, too. 'Yeah. They probably just forgot.'

That, of course, made Jamie feel worse. Alex obviously felt he'd gone a bit far and said, 'They probably just expect you to be there.'

'You reckon?' Jamie bounced back in an instant. Personally, I would have left him squirming a bit longer, but Alex has always been a bit of a softie.

And so it went on. Somehow, Alex, with a little help from me, managed to give Jamie a whole picture of a party at Sasha's place (nicely timed to coincide with her planned seduction of Rob. I may have to give him to her in the end, but not without a fight).

It wasn't just any party, oh no. It was fancy dress, with the theme of 'Loony Tunes' cartoons. Jamie decided immediately that he would be Bugs Bunny.

Afterwards, Al felt a bit bad.

'The thing is, Sooz, making Jamie look like a prat is so easy it's the same as taking sweeties from a baby. I feel mean. And there's another thing. If this is the top chance for Sasha and Rob to get back together, should we be getting in the way?'

You betcha, pal, I thought. But Al doesn't know my plans for Rob, so I just smiled.

'But Alex,' I said, 'he asked for it. Begged for it. It'll teach him to keep his sticky beak out of other people's business. And I expect he's ordered his bunny suit already. He's looking forward to dressing up...'

Al's conscience is thankfully a very small one, and the mental picture of Sasha, swinging open her front door with her best seductive smile to find Bugs Bunny leering at her, was just too good to resist.

So we left it. We sneaked round to Sasha's and hid in the bushes so we could see Jamie arrive. He looked magnificent. If there had been a female bunny within half a mile, he would have pulled, no question. He was so into character, he even *hopped* up to the front door.

Some poor old lady walking her Pekinese nearly had a heart attack. I think she thought the bunny was going to mug her, 'cos she screamed and dropped the dog's lead. The dog was too fat and too stupid to run away, though. Jamie calmly picked up the lead, handed it back to the old dear and hopped on his way. I bet she'll never take a glass of sherry of an evening again.

We fell out of the bushes laughing, which didn't help her state of mind at all. I've never seen a crumbly move so fast.

It was a cheap laugh, but a good one. Didn't work, though. Despite having Jamie in a bunny suit being a king-sized gooseberry at their little love tryst, Rob and Sasha still managed to get back together. And Jamie isn't talking to Alex at all. He's barely snarling at me. Apparently, he 'expects that kind of thing from you, Sooz. But Alex is supposed to be a mate.' Well cheers, I thought *I* was supposed to be a mate as well. But I keep forgetting, I don't have a penis and I'm not hot tottie either. These are the qualifications for the chosen ones.

How was I supposed to know this was Sasha's idea of romantic?

Do you have times when you look at your mates and wonder what the hell you're doing with them? Sometimes I think, if they're your friends, Jamie old son, thank the stars you don't have enemies. There's no way I would have led my best friend up the garden path the way Alex did. He set me up for mega-humiliation, and didn't even say sorry. As for Sooz... well, I suppose you have to expect that sort of thing from Sooz. She's about as friendly as a spiny anteater. But I thought we were good enough mates for her to come to my rescue. Sure, she likes to push it a bit. But to let me head off dressed in full bunny gear to crash a hot seduction scene which Sasha had planned for lover boy Rob? Now *that's* betrayal.

jamie

I can't believe I fell for it; they must think I'm a right puppethead. But why would I suspect that two of my very best mates would set me up? Anyway, I show up at Sasha's dressed as a rabbit, for the fancy-dress party Al and Sooz tell me is happening. In the process I nearly give an old lady in the street a heart attack. It's not every day you see a 1.8-metre bunny blocking your way on the pavement. And when I get to the flat I find Sasha, dressed up like a dog's dinner with lips so full of kiss-me gloss I almost try to snog her – *at it like a rabbit*, see? Getting into character.

I don't know who was most annoyed, her or me. Well, her I think. But as I was there, I tried to make the best of it. I didn't know she was planning to get Rob alone and have her wicked way with him. At the time, I thought she needed cheering up. There were no proper lights on, just candles all over the place, and really slow music on the CD player. It was like being in a funeral parlour. I thought she must be feeling really low. Turns out it was her version of romantic.

Then I saw the dips. People in deep depression don't cut up little carrot sticks and prepare dips, do they? That's when I twigged it must be a man.

jamie

'You look well guilty,' I said. 'It's a man. You've got a man coming over.'

She couldn't deny it. She looked upset. Clearly a woman in need of advice, I thought. And even though I had been expecting a party and obviously wasn't going to get one, I generously decided to give her the benefit of my experience. I thought it would be good practice for the book I'm writing, too.

Sash looked kinda fidgety, and said she didn't need advice. She more or less tried to bundle me out of the door, but I wasn't having it. 'So, Sash,' I said, 'do I know this chap you're gonna be romancing tonight?'

I could tell by the way that she went all silent that I'd scored the home run. It had to be Rob or Alex. And it was hardly going to be Alex, right?

Sure enough, a couple of minutes later the doorbell rings and what do you know? Rob. Surprise, surprise.

The atmosphere was a bit strained, to say the least. When I told Sooz about it later, she said, 'What do you expect, Jamie? Rob comes round expecting a twosome with Sasha and a chance to sort out their problems and he finds you in a bunny suit tucking into his dips!'

But she wasn't there, so what does she know?

jamie

*The air was charged with sexual tension, as well it
might be between a long-term couple who'd never
had sex. My first task as their adviser and counsellor
was to lower the emotional temperature.*

That's how I'm going to write it in my book. I want to
include a few practical examples of how my wisdom and
experience have been called upon. I was willing to cancel
my cab and make a night of it, but Rob and Sasha insisted they'd be all right on their own. So I did my best to
make conversation while I waited, to get them started.

I thought it would be best to try and avoid any topic
that could lead back to sex. That was something they
needed to talk over in private. But how many things could
you talk about that didn't have sex in them, given that a
healthy young male thinks about sex every six seconds?

'Did you know,' I said, 'that in 1899 the average speed
of motorized transport was 12 miles an hour?'

Rob closed his eyes. Sasha gave me a weird look.
They're thawing a bit, I thought. Well done, Jamie.

'And now, twenty years later, the twenty-first century,
it's the same... 12 miles an hour!'

Trying to keep a conversation going was a real strain.

Neither Sash nor Rob made much effort. But I did my best to keep them interested, and by the time my cab arrived they were a bit more relaxed. They both came to see me off, and hauled me into the cab (my bunny ears got stuck, unfortunately).

'Only because they couldn't wait to get rid of you,' said Sooz. Little Miss Sad-sack, as usual.

Whatever Sooz says, I think I was able to help them. Sasha and Rob are back together now, so that's proof enough, right?

But don't go thinking that means I'm gonna forgive Alex for what he did. Never cross a man with a mind as keen and sharp as Jamie Collier's, my friend. Jamie Collier *always* settles the score. Just wait.

jamie

MAKEPEACE MANURE PRODUCTS LTD.

Hanover Terrace
Stuart Lane
Essex CH2 7BD

Phone: 0208 779365
Fax: 0208 779366
Email: moremuck@blimey.co

Invoice

Invoice #: 75890/975
Invoice Date: 22Nov

Bill To:

Alex Dunbar
33, Backman Road
Waltham Cross,
Essex

Makepeace—More Manure for Your Money!

DATE	YOUR ORDER #	OUR ORDER #	SALES REP.	FOB	SHIP VIA	TERMS	TAX ID
17 November	123	9876/01/229	Barry Witlow	INTERNET order		14 days	N/a

QUANTITY	ITEM	UNITS	DESCRIPTION	DISCOUNT %	TAXABLE	UNIT PRICE	TOTAL
3	Manure	10k bags	Best quality garden manure: liquid	X	X	£12.99	£38.97

Special Delivery Instructions. Leave

on doorstep if customer not home

Subtotal	£38.97
Tax	X
Delivery Charge	£10.00
Miscellaneous	X
Balance Due	£48.97

Have you grown a penis?

I have done some pretty stupid things in my time, while I've been growing up. Who hasn't? But I hope I will never do anything as stupid as the stuff Alex has been up to these last few weeks.

It turns out he's been seeing a policeman. By 'seeing', I mean a fair bit more than visual contact. I mean the kind of 'seeing' that is illegal until you're eighteen, if you're a guy. The kind that can have you up in court if you're the one 'seeing' someone under eighteen, and the kind that will certainly end up with you losing your job and maybe much worse, if you happen to be a copper.

What was Alex thinking of? He tells me and Sooz it's love, but come on. Alex isn't thick. He must have realized what the implications would be for Dan if he was

jamie

caught having it off with a seventeen-year-old. But he didn't stop. Instead, he told Dan, his policeman boyfriend, that he was twenty. Big lie. Bad, selfish lie. Love? I don't think so.

There are lots of things about this that freak me. One, the thought that Alex has risked going to jail and, worse, has risked his boyfriend going to jail and losing his job. Two, that Alex used me and Sooz as part of his cover. We could be dragged down with him, if it all goes pear-shaped. That's not what friends are for, Alex.

Sooz and I only found out about all this when the computers got nicked from college. Naturally the police came along to investigate. Enter Dan, the policeman. Apparently he bumped into Alex in the corridor and expressed predictable surprise at seeing Jamie, the twenty-year-old I.T. consultant, hanging out at a Sixth Form College. So Alex, never one to be fazed by an awkward situation, immediately tells Dan he's on the college staff, does the odd lecture, would you believe.

The first I get to hear about this is when I'm in the loo at college, just about to do what comes naturally when Alex and Sooz (yes, Sooz) barge me into a cubicle and lock themselves in with me. At the time I was so shocked

jamie

it didn't seem at all unnatural to see Sooz, who often claims to be a female, hanging out in the gents'.

'I need a favour,' said Alex.

Straight in, no messing about with, 'Sorry I stopped you in mid-flow, Jamie. I'll be sure to pay all the bills when you end up with prostate problems because of the shock, Jamie.'

I was a bit peeved, to be honest. *He* may have forgotten how he humiliated me in the bunny suit episode. I haven't.

'I need a favour,' he says. Bloody cheek.

'You're in no position to ask,' I say, but Sooz is nosier than me.

'What kind of favour?'

'I'm up to my neck!' Alex looks strange, a bit scared, even. 'It's Dan.'

I'm mystified. 'Dan?'

'Boyfriend,' supplies Sooz helpfully, as if I didn't know. 'He's here...'

That's when Alex dropped his little bombshell about being a copper's bit of underage love interest.

'I told him I was in I.T., troubleshooting, installing software... I told him I was twenty.'

jamie

Picture the scene. Me, Sooz and Alex locked in a public loo together, discussing his illegal love life. Sooz and I were so gobsmacked we could hardly breathe. Or maybe that was the fumes. Sorry. Always make stupid jokes when I'm nervous.

Sooz, as usual, was quicker on the uptake than me.

'So, he could get done for... with a minor?'

My God, I thought, so he could. What would they do to a policeman, I wondered, who turned out to be not only gay (I've got a fair idea what police think about gays on the whole) but having a fling with a seventeen-year-old college boy? And what about me and Sooz? If we knew, and helped Alex to hide it (you could see from his face what he was going to ask), did that make us accomplices? Would we be aiding and abetting a crime?

'Guys, you've got to back me up if he sees me,' said Alex. He looked in a right panic.

'What, say you're Mister Grown-up Computer Man?' I almost laughed, but I could see he was dead serious.

'You're walking a fine line,' I told him. I know I sounded like Miss Brogden, our primary school teacher, but I meant it. 'You owe me big-time, Alex.'

jamie

'Don't owe me, I'm loving it,' said Sooz straight away. Trust Sooz, I thought. And that was the moment it hit me.

Our Sooz, in the men's.

'*Men's* toilet,' I said, as pointedly as I could. 'Have you grown a penis?'

Quick as the wind, she bit back. 'No. Have you?'

Sooz just doesn't have the kind of boundaries normal people have. Whatever poor sod gets her as a girlfriend, if ever such a sucker comes along, will have to live in a state of permanent high alert for embarrassment. And he'll probably always have a plaster or a bandage on. Sooz can be very physical when she's angry.

Anyway, no sooner had we sworn undying oaths of loyalty and secrecy, and exited the gents', than who should come along but Dan? Alex literally walked into him.

'What you doing here?'

Someone had to do something, and fast. For once, I was ahead of Sooz.

'Excuse me, Mr Stanton. I was wondering if you had that computer book you were telling us about?'

Alex looked like a rabbit caught in headlights. Given the way he had humiliated me just days before with the rabbit suit incident, I have to admit it gave me just one moment of pure, joyful satisfaction.

Sooz lunged in, looking half-crazed (I think she was trying to look keen and enthusiastic, but that's like asking your parents to stop nagging – too alien to be possible).

'Eh?' said Alex.

'Last week,' said Sooz.

It was a prompt; it gave Alex a chance.

'Oh, sure, yeah,' he said.

Me and Sooz smiled like grateful little students, and Alex sauntered off.

Didn't do him any good, though. He bumped into Dan again at the end of the investigation. Alex had used the computer room, see, and had to make a statement. Dan came into the room just as Alex was telling Dan's fellow officer his date of birth. Well, the police know how to tot up that kind of maths, don't they? Must have taken Dan all of a split second to work out that he and Alex were suddenly on the wrong side of the law. He must be bricking it right now.

Thing is, I'm angry with Alex, but I haven't shown it. Quite the opposite, in fact. I've tried to comfort the bastard.

'You told a few white lies,' I said. 'Who hasn't?'

jamie

Then I gave him the good old plenty-more-fish-in-the-sea speech. But all the time, I was angry. Alex saw Dan in a gym, and fancied him. He wanted Dan, and he didn't think past the wanting, or consider what might happen to Dan if they were caught. No way is that love. He didn't think how it might all come down on his mates, either. Selfish, all the way.

Sometimes, I wish I was like Sooz. If she's angry, she'll tell you so. She's brave, fearless, stands up for what she believes even when it makes her unpopular. She doesn't care about anything.

But I only wish I was like Sooz when I'm feeling gutless, like now, and could do with a bit of her courage. I wouldn't want her looks. Or her dress sense. Or her ability to put people's backs up. Or, let's face it, her tattoos and nose ring.

jamie

Nothing stops me when I'm like this.

Alex is in deep doo-doo. Not that he doesn't deserve it, and if there's any justice in the world he'll suffer a lot more yet. But I do feel sorry for him.

Last night, when I saw him in the café looking so crushed, I just wanted to cry for him. I didn't, of course. I hit him instead.

'You can wipe that look off your face,' I said. 'You've got off bloody lightly, for what you've done. Call that love? Selfish sex-mad queer is what you are, not tragic victim. So don't try that with me.'

I don't know where it all came from. I wanted to be sympathetic, give him a shoulder to cry on. Alex is a good mate, whatever he's done. I am such a screw-up these days that even when I try to express sympathy it comes out like an explosion from hell.

sooz

Jamie was there. He squirmed and looked the other way.

'None of the blokes I know would go near you for a bet.'

He was trying to cheer Alex up, encouraging him to talk. I clenched my fists, dug my nails into my palms, bit my lip. But nothing stops me when I'm like this.

'You're a complete bastard,' I told Alex. 'Dragging everyone you claim to care about into your sordid little life.' Then I stomped off to get a coffee from Rob, who eyed me nervously, as if he was thinking I might turn on him next.

'There's nothing sexy about being the bitch from hell, is there?'

Jamie's a better friend than me. I'm a flat-chested freak with the social skills of a moron and a temper I can't control. Sometimes, I feel so worthless and stupid and angry with myself that it just sort of explodes. Then it hurts whoever happens to be near enough to catch the fall-out.

I'm a fully paid-up member of the totally screwed-up society of complete and utter nutters. I'll be alone all my life, because there's no one out there screwy enough to put up with me.

Meanwhile, I've got to somehow put things right with Alex. Jamie thinks I'm the bitch from hell for what I said to Alex – kicking him when he's down, Jamie said. I don't know why I should care about that, but I do. A bit, anyway.

Wedding invitation

The marriage of Angela Berryman
and John Braithwaite

Will take place at St Mary's Church, London W1
and afterwards at Swankies, Mayfair.
They would be delighted if

Could join them on this happy day

Date: 17th September

Time: 2 p.m.

RSVP
Mr and Mrs Arthur Berryman, 39
Gracechurch Avenue,
Benfleet, Hants

Looks innocent enough, yeah? Simple invitation to a simple wedding (and they don't come much simpler than my cousin). But I've lived in this family all my life; I know what it's really about.

My cousin Becky, of the dull hairstyle, dorky fiancé and safe-but-boring job:

Mustn't forget to invite Sooz, poor thing. Maybe seeing me with a man will encourage her to try a bit harder.

My aunty, who shops exclusively by mail order and has trouble with her bunions so tries to pretend her slippers are a fashion statement:

I suppose we'll have to invite Susan, I don't want to cause a family rift.

I bet there was a tactful telephone conversation with Mum about the 'companion'. Nothing as obvious as, *Has poor Sooz managed to get herself a man yet?* And my mum, ever the optimist:

Yes, I'm sure Sooz will want to bring someone...

So the invitations went out, and even as they were licking the envelopes and leaving smears of cheap lipstick, they were wondering what on earth Sooz might wear to the wedding and which planet she'd have to trawl to find a date.

I know all this because I've had one of *those* conversations with my mother.

'What are you going to wear, Sooz, dear?' Not so much a question as a warning.

'Actually, Mum, I probably won't be able to go. Loads of coursework due, you know.'

Worth a try.

'What nonsense. If you've got time to gad about with those friends of yours, you've time to go to your cousin's wedding. It's a family occasion. I'll have none of your little moods. Now, I saw a lovely tailored suit in one of your aunty's catalogues...'

Gad about... little moods... tailored suits? You'd never guess my mum spends most of her time watching Fifties movies, would you?

It was a matter of pride. I had to find a suitable man. Someone gorgeous enough to shut them up once and for all. And if my cousins were jealous, that would be an added bonus. The problem is, the number of gorgeous blokes I know can be counted on the finger of a one-fingered person. And I didn't think Rob would agree to it, even if Sasha let him out of her clutches.

As always, I went to Alex.

'A wedding? All day? With your family?'

The tone wasn't hopeful.

'Yeah,' I said, trying to be upbeat. 'Free food, free booze, disco, a chance to gain an insight into other people's lives...'

'Sooz. Your family don't have lives. Your family are so boring they make *mine* look good.'

'Not very tactful, Alex.'

'True, though.'

I nodded. Fair enough.

'So, will you come?'

Alex put his arm around my shoulder. 'Look Sooz, ordinarily I would love to give up a whole day to hang out with your family discussing the winter frost on your dad's Brussels sprouts and your cousin's acne problem. It would be a treat to see you trying to pretend you weren't related to any of them while your mum pumped me for info about how far we've gone and your brother got drunk enough to handle the karaoke...'

'How do you know there'll be karaoke?'

'Sooz, I've been to your family stuff loads of times. There's *always* karaoke. Your dad always gets drunk and sings "My Way" and you always blackmail him when he's sobered up and found out you have a video of it all...'

'Yeah, yeah, all right. So will you go, or is there a but coming up?'

Alex smiled. 'Sorry, Sooz. Hot date. Ask Jamie. He loves a good karaoke. And he's got a suit.'

'I'll ask Jamie, yeah – when there are no other guys left on this entire planet and my whole family has been struck with a terrible virus that means they can't see or hear anything. Then I'll take Jamie, and pretend he's gorgeous-looking and says incredibly witty things...'

'Like me, you mean?' Alex looked dead chuffed.

'No, not at all like you. That's the beauty of pretend, isn't it? In pretend, I could take someone who's *really* good-looking.'

I tried everyone I could think of. Not many. I even sank to the level of asking the gawky computer nerd in the year below me who used to follow me about a bit. But he's got a girlfriend now. Time to believe in miracles.

I'm out of ideas and phone numbers. I either get desperate and advertise in the Lonely Hearts column, which someone in my family might see, or get truly desperate and ask Jamie. Tough choice. Total humiliation, or total humiliation? You decide...

SOOZ

And my mum has always liked you...

She thrust the invitation under my nose and said, 'What do you think?'

'Not your kind of gig,' I said.

'I've got to go, though, it's my cousin.' Sooz slumped onto the bench and threw her head back. The sun hit her nose ring full on. It made me feel a bit queasy.

'What do you think could be more boring than a traditional wedding with your whole family there watching your primary school teacher cousin marrying the assistant building society manager geek?' she asked.

It was a challenge. I put my brain into gear.

'A lecture on quantum mechanics?'

'Nope,' she said.

'Listening to Nicki and Sasha talking about make-up?

jamie

No, wait, that's a bit of a turn-on, actually...'

'You're sick, Jamie.'

'A weekend with the caravan club?'

'Closer,' she nodded. 'Thing is, Jamie, I've got to go and I've even got to try and look what Mum calls "normal".'

I sat up and turned to look at her properly, trying to imagine what changes her mum would have to make. The hair would have to go, I could see that. Sooz spends hours twisting those dreadlocks and dying them just the right colour combinations. She wouldn't be happy about ditching all that effort and going for a girlie bob.

Then there was all the metal. She might get away with one earring in each ear and one or two things around her neck. But you know Sooz. She's sort of studded all over. Chokers, nose ring, eyebrow piercing, lip stud. Probably all sorts of other bits of metal in places she'd thump me for looking at. And the make-up? It would be interesting to see what her eyes are like under all that black stuff.

Sooz saw me looking. 'What?' she said. Her eyes had that dangerous sparkly look. 'What?!'

Everyone chooses a look that says who they are, don't they? Whether it's geek or cool dude, religious nutter or sex bomb, you can sort of tell with most people by looking.

jamie

Well with Sooz, it's like that plus 300 per cent. Sooz and her look are two halves of the same thing. Take away Sooz's clothes and studs and make-up, and you may as well peel off her skin. You had to feel sorry for her.

On the other hand, I couldn't erase a picture in my head of Sooz in a plain woollen skirt and a nice white blouse, with proper, feminine tights and no make-up. Maybe a touch of mascara, bit of lip gloss. She's probably got quite nice eyes under all that lot. Wouldn't mind seeing the real Sooz underneath the paint. (And taking a picture so's I could forever hold it over her when she's being a cow...)

'Sooz, why don't you just say you can't go? Say you've got an essay due in. Or throw a sickie on the day.'

'My mum's got a radar for sickies.' Sooz aimed a vicious kick at a can lying near the bench.

'Ouch!' A passing student glared at her.

She glared back.

'Sorry!' I called out.

Sooz glared at me.

'It's a three-line whip,' she said. 'I've got to go. And look!' She thrust the card at me again and stabbed the word 'companion'. 'You know what that's about, don't you?'

jamie

I peered at the card. 'They want you to bring some-one?'

'Yes. And why?'

I thought it must be a trick question. I looked at it from every angle. But I couldn't see any answer except the obvious.

'Um, they want you to bring a friend so's you'll have a good time?'

Sooz snorted and whacked me one across the ear. Not hard, but only because she couldn't be bothered to make the effort.

'They want to see whether poor old Sooz can whistle up any kind of man. Probably not, they're thinking, but let's give her a chance. It'll give us something to gossip about either way.'

'Sooz, it doesn't say bring a man. It says bring a *companion.* You could just as easily take a girlfriend.' I felt quite chuffed that I'd spotted something Sooz hadn't. Usually she's ahead of me, though I'd never admit that in public.

She groaned. 'Jamie, you are such an arse,' she said. 'Of course it means male companion. God, if I showed up with a woman that really *would* set the tongues wagging, wouldn't it?'

jamie

I gave up. Always best, with Sooz.

'Who you going to take, then? Alex?'

Alex does a nice sideline in pretending to be a boyfriend when a girl is in a bit of a fix. He's exactly the kind of scrubbed, respectable young man mothers approve of. So when his lesbian friends need to keep parents off their back, or when someone's got the kind of man parents would go ape about, Alex is the stooge. It's in his interests, because then he has a ready supply of phoney girlfriends to keep *his* parents off the scent. Not Sooz, though. His mum would rather find out he was gay than think he was going around with Sooz.

'I thought *you* might like a day out,' she said.

'What? *Me*?'

I made an elaborate show of looking surprised. I wasn't. Alex told me about her trawling the campus asking just about everyone. I was expecting her to come to me, in the end. She always does.

'Why me?'

'You look better in a suit than Alex.'

There was no arguing with that.

'And my mum has always liked you...'

jamie

I wasn't sure if this was a good or a bad thing in Sooz's eyes.

'And...' Sooz started.

'And I've got the kind of style that you need to be seen with, to impress people,' I finished for her. I wondered how low she was prepared to crawl.

Not that low, obviously.

'And Alex has a hot date lined up,' Sooz said.

'I'm not sure if I'm available that weekend,' I said. I didn't want Sooz to think I was so sad I didn't have as many options as Alex. 'I might have a date lined up myself. I'll have to check.'

'No need,' said Sooz. 'I'll tell you exactly what your choices are that day. Being a sad tosser loafing about watching telly and going down the café, or a sad tosser loafing about watching telly and meeting up with other sad tossers down the pub. Go on, Jamie. Say yes. The food will be really good. And the drink will be free. We might even be able to smuggle some decent music in for the disco. And if it's really bad, we'll sneak off early and go the multiplex. I'll even pay. Yeah?'

For Sooz, that's mega-generosity on a stick.

The upshot is, I agreed. I'm going to this family

jamie

wedding with Sooz. She won't talk about what she's wearing. All she says is, 'Nothing special.'

But that's just a line. All girls dress up for weddings, don't they? And I've been having this dream about picking Sooz up in my Ferrari (in a dream you can have what you want, no prob). She's wearing one of those off-the-shoulder silk things, with lovely sparkly eyes and straight, shiny hair. And high heels. Maybe even fishnet tights underneath. In the dream, I'm really like, 'Wow!' And she smiles, a proper, girlie smile. And I lean forward to kiss her...

And then I wake up in a cold sweat. 'Cos even in a silk dress, she'd still be Sooz, friend to the great white shark. If ever Sooz does get someone mad enough to mate with her, you just know she'll eat him afterwards. In a pie, probably.

jamie

I just didn't know where to put myself.

As days out go, this one had to be right up there with having your teeth pulled. All of them. Without anaesthetic. A white wedding, complete with candy-floss bride, pink giggly brides-maids and a gawky groom who cried – *cried* – during his speech. My mum cried, too, but that was only when I took my coat off and she saw that underneath I did *not have* the little suit she'd bought me from Marks & Spencers 'as a treat'. You've got to admire her nerve, I suppose.

Jamie, of course, fits right in with my family. My Aunty Barbara said it was nice to see me settling down with such a nice young man at last. Jamie beamed like a little kid with a huge lollipop, and I was forced to kick him.

Becky the bride batted her eyelashes at Jamie and simpered that she hoped I would catch the bridal bouquet (no chance — I'd rather be bound and gagged). The groom, who prides himself on being a bit of a reader, made a couple of feeble jokes about *The Taming of the Shrew* that were not at all complimentary.

Jamie, bless him, said, 'Oh, Sooz isn't a shrew at all.' Which I thought was sweet. Until he followed it with, 'She's more like a cross between a great white shark and a barracuda. The shrew turned into a proper wife in the end, didn't she? Can't catch Sooz doing that...'

I had to kick him again to shut him up; the groom disappeared fast 'cos he could see he might be next.

My gran was telling everyone what a lovely couple we make. Everyone, including the vicar, the waiters, an old guy in the bar with his dog... and a good-looking bloke I might have stood a chance with, if Jamie hadn't been hanging around playing the part of my boyfriend so enthusiastically. I know I wanted to pretend, but it's insulting, all the same. Do they think I've got no taste whatsoever? The best you could say about Jamie is that it was better to have him there than to go alone and be pitied.

I know that's not fair. At least Jamie tries. My mum and the groom's mum were even swapping apple pie recipes at one stage. I just didn't know where to put myself. Nobody showed a single milligram of imagination or creativity. The local shops must have had a field day when that lot went shopping for their outfits. 'Come on, Brenda, you have one of those in beige, and the pink'll do me. Now, what about those three-for-the-price-of-two hats over there?'

Jamie chatted to everyone. He sounded a bit like a slightly spaced-out granddad at a family reunion:

'Uncle Bernie, Uncle Bernie... yeah, I remember. You're the one who builds swimming pools, right? Is that indoors or outdoors, usually?'

'She's gorgeous? How old is she? Nearly one... be walking soon, then.'

He did bend his elbow a bit hard at the reception when the champagne came round. But by then the speeches were in full swing. Straight up, you had to be half-pickled or die. They were good speeches, but you can have too much of a good thing. None of the speakers recognized that 'enough' moment when it came.

Once the band 'struck up a tune' as my dad called it, we knew we had to leave.

It was too late for the film. We bought a huge bag of chips and sat on a bench. That was probably the best part of the day, chomping on chips and reliving the highlights.

'What did you think of the dress, Sooz?'

'Wouldn't wash my windows with it. What about you?'

'It was all right, in a girlie sort of way. It matched that ludicrous velvet suit and frilly shirt your brother-in-law was wearing.'

'They really did go for total puffball candy, didn't they?' I said.

Jamie nodded and lay back, his head on my lap. Almost sweet, except for the blob of ketchup on his chin with a bit of chip in it.

'Not my kind of wedding,' said Jamie.

'Nor mine. What would you go for?'

Jamie sat up and attempted to look thoughtful. Not an easy task.

'I'd go off quietly to the register office one day without telling anyone...'

'What, kidnap the girl and carry her off in a sack?'

'Not anyone except the bride, obviously, and a couple of really close mates for witnesses. And afterwards I'd throw a huge party, invite everyone and tell them what we'd done. That's my kind of wedding.'

I was shocked. That's exactly what I would do. I pushed him off my lap and hit him. 'Look what you've done with that ketchup, you're disgusting.'

'What, you're not going to marry me, then?' He tried to snuggle up.

'You what? For God's sake, Jamie, sober up or your mum will kill you.'

'Why did you run after the bouquet, then?'

'I did not! I was trying to get out of the way! How was I supposed to know Becky is the talk of the Willington Ladies Rugby Club for the strength of her throw-ins?'

'You still caught it, though.' He had that smug look he always has when he's completely rat-arsed and feeling superior.

'Jamie, when two tons of flowers come hurtling out of space at you, you try to shield yourself. Those flowers literally fell into my arms.'

'If you say so...' Jamie gave me a knowing wink.

There's no point in trying to talk sense to Jamie when he's drunk – or at any other time, come to think of it, so I let it go. We sat in silence a while, thinking about the day.

Now I look back on it, most of it was a good laugh. But if I was going to get married, which I wouldn't want to and anyway I haven't even got a boyfriend so the chances are a bit slim, but if I ever were to think about it, Cousin Becky's wedding would be a list of everything I didn't want. It's such a load of bull, all that froth and daft speeches. My mum and dad would only be invited if they promised to keep their mouths shut and not carp or criticize (and let me choose their clothes). And there'd be a live band, not a disco, playing all the stuff me and Jamie like...

Jamie? How the hell did his name come up? Slip of the tongue, that's all. We're good mates, there's no reason he shouldn't come to my wedding, is there? But Jamie is the last person on earth I would marry. He might be cute, and funny. And he may be one of the few people you can really count on when the chips are down. But he's still Jamie, the one-stop shop for everything you need for your partner from hell.

This bouquet must have had a homing device.

The wedding thing wasn't as much of a bore as I'd expected. But Sooz had made it sound like such a nightmare it could never have been as bad in reality. When I went round to meet her I was still caught up in the dream about her in a silk dress, looking all sort of gorgeous and feminine. Fat chance. I knew as soon as she let me in – wearing her coat, on a warm day – that she was not what her mum would call 'suitably attired for a wedding'. Either her mum hadn't noticed in the last-minute panic, or she's a bit thick. Or totally defeated. 'Cos she beamed at me, happy as a bonking bunny, and went off to call a taxi.

'Sooz, you look...' I know you're supposed to say how great a girl looks but Sooz looked the same as always. Actually that was a relief. I couldn't have handled the

jamie

Sooz from my dream. She did have a new nose stud – a little sapphire. 'Your new stud's cute,' I said.

'Cute?' Sooz almost spat the word out. 'You sound like my mother.' She stomped past me and went outside.

Sooz didn't take her coat off until we got to the reception. Then I saw she was wearing exactly the same stuff she wears down to the coffee bar or to college. She hadn't dressed up at all, just tied her hair back and bought a new stud.

'Sooz!' Her mum was shocked, a bit tearful. Sooz just shrugged, and pulled me over to our table.

'You could have made a bit of an effort, Sooz,' I hissed at her. 'I'm wearing a bloody suit!'

'More fool you, then,' she said.

Sooz's family are pleasant, ordinary people who must think Sooz was dropped off by an alien force. They were all really nice and easy to get along with. Not one of them thumped me, or made sarky comments. Where does she get it from?

The wedding wasn't my kind of thing, but the food was good and they didn't stinge on the booze. We escaped as soon as we could. We bought chips and slagged off the whole wedding: bride, groom, clothes, speeches, music, the works. We should have felt bad about it, but we didn't. Too drunk, possibly.

It'll be a great day to look back on. And we'll be able to share it with all our friends because I took a camera. I've got pics of Sooz dancing with her dorky cousin and trying to force a friendly smile. They'll love that, down at the café. But there's even better. When the time came for the bride to throw her bouquet, Sooz started pushing to the back of the crowd, trying to escape. But just as Becky threw it, someone called her name. She turned round, and I swear this bouquet must have had a homing device or something (wouldn't put anything past her mother). Sooz sees it coming through the air towards her and *instinctively catches it*.

God bless fast film. I managed to get two or three shots, and captured the whole thing. Sooz was too shocked to notice. Everyone cheered, and she dropped it like a hot brick and ran. She doesn't know about the pics. I'm not so stupid as to let on I had a camera. She'll cripple me when she finds out, but hopefully not before I've shown them to everyone. Or maybe I'll just keep them for blackmail. Might come in handy. What d'ya reckon?

jamie

LUST, LOVE, LIFE

JAMIE COLLIER

The bestselling 'how to' manual for the successful man in a woman-dominated world

contents

introduction

This book's my way of trying to pass on a few tips to guys less fortunate than me. Pulling a bird is not just to do with sexual attraction. Women go for something a bit more than muscles and a six-pack (although these are, of course, important, and I wouldn't be where I am today without a reasonable score in *that* department). No, these days women want someone who is warm, sensitive and caring. Someone who is interested (or pretends to be) in what's going on in *their* lives. They probably won't share your passion for the local footie team, or think that sinking fourteen pints in one sitting is a real accomplishment. They want wit, humour and a willingness to shop.

It was a hard path for me, in my younger days. I feel sorry for lads who are just starting out. We're all looking for that first experience that will set us on the path to a permanent relationship. Failing that, we want at least a steady supply of experiments while we sort out who the right person might be. So I have written this book as a sort of short cut. In it I have put all the things I have learned from women, and from men, about how to get and keep a girlfriend. I hope it works for you. If it does, pass it on. Men should stick together and support each other. It's not just for the girlies. It can work for us too.

What do you reckon? It's only a rough draft of course. At first I thought it was a bit preachy, you know, more like a sermon in church than a self-help book. So I tried to give it a sort of mates-in-the-pub tone. I'm quite pleased with it.

I'm not going to show it to anyone until it's finished and on sale in the bookshops. They'd spoil it. Sooz wouldn't be able to resist pointing out that I haven't even *got* a girlfriend, and that I've never, ever *kept* one. I can hear her now.

'Who taught you the most, Jamie? That one-night stand you picked up at Louise's party when you were so drunk you freaked out and phoned Rob to come and rescue you when you woke up? Or Nicki, perhaps – you got on like a house on fire there, didn't you? Only trouble was, she set fire to the house with you in it...'

Sooz always brings out the wet blanket when she thinks someone else might be heading for success.

What Sooz and the others don't understand is that advice in a book and real life have nothing to do with each other. Does a politician in charge of family policy stay faithful to his wife? No, otherwise a lot of newspapers would have nothing for the front page. Teachers are forever telling their students how important it is to keep ahead with assignments – but are they ever ahead with lecture preparation? Of course not. They rush in at the last minute with papers falling all over the place and pathetic excuses about the photocopier breaking down. Your mum witters on about how unhealthy it is to eat so many burgers and chips. Then *she* settles down to watch the telly with chocolates and a cream bun.

Need I go on? The fact is, knowing what people *should* be doing is one skill, and being able to make *yourself* do what you know people should be doing is another, different, totally unrelated skill. I've got the one and I'm still developing the other.

jamie

how to pull

In this section of the book I have drawn on years of experience and observation to offer guidelines as to how to get a woman interested, get her to go out with you and, if all goes well, get her to come up with a bit more than a goodnight kiss.

First, and most important to remember, is **respect**. Women are very big on this. If they think you're just trying to get into their knickers, you stand no chance. So remember to take things slowly. By all means have a good snog at the end of the first date, but don't try to take things any further until you've been out at least three or four times. Unless she seems keen, of course, when it's every man for himself.

Second is **cleanliness**. Good looks are important, but you can look like a love god and still get nowhere if you haven't made the effort in the bathroom. Shave before you meet, and try to match your shower gel and aftershave. To get some idea of what the best brands are, cruise around Boots and see which ones have the trendiest displays. But remember to look in your dad's bathroom cabinet so you know what to avoid. You don't want a girl to think she's snogging an old man. And don't forget to clean your teeth and slap on the deodorant. Some women like the rough and rugged types, but most won't get into any kind of clinch with them until they've had a bath.

A good **chat-up line** is a must. 'I really fancy you, do you want to go out with me?' might be straightforward, but it's only likely to work with a girl who's desperate for a bloke. And it won't do your image any good at all to be seen with someone like that. No, there needs to be a bit of a challenge. You must win the hand of the lady, just like the chivalrous knights that you see in films (but without the poncey hair and horses).

Good chat-up lines, once you've found them, should be kept secret and not shared with anyone. But I am prepared to divulge one or two for the purposes of instruction. Try these:

Hi. I got nothin' to do and lots of time to do it in. Would you like to join me?

You're the kind of person I wouldn't mind being stuck in an avalanche with. What say we kick up a snow-storm together?

Try to be suave and sophisticated in the delivery of the line. Think James Bond. Not Mr Bean.

Flowers or chocolates are very important in those first few approaches. Dishing them out on the first date shows you really appreciate the woman going out with you. But don't do it too often, or you'll look easy.

Women are very contradictory and difficult to judge. On the one hand they like a touch of the masterful 'treat 'em mean, keep 'em keen' stuff, but if you take it too far they whinge about you not being romantic and taking them for granted. So do it on the first date, and then maybe every three months or so (if you stay together that long). And always buy flowers or chocolates after a row. If it's your fault, buy both. If it's not your fault, just buy one, but apologize anyway. Ask yourself, what's more important, truth and honesty or being able to get your leg over at the end of the night? Enough said.

Finally, a word of caution. Never try to pull a bird when you're out with your **mates, drinking.** Only desperate women go for drunken men (see above). And in any case, if you're with your mates there's a good chance one of them will fancy the woman you're after. You don't want to end up competing, even if you think you could win. A girlfriend is usually temporary and a mate is much more permanent. Mates shouldn't fight over women – but they shouldn't share them, either. That makes life complicated.

It's going well, innit? I can't wait till it's published, to see if any of this stuff really works.

You looked like you enjoyed it to me.

Immature, stupid little children. We think we're so cool, so grown-up. We're nothing more than kiddies with a dressing-up box and Mummy's make-up.

Whose idea was it to play truth or dare? I can't even remember. Nicki or Sasha, it had to be. Sometimes it's hard to believe people like those two exist at all, never mind exist in a world where people like them and think they're funny. The hurt they make together just goes on and on. Especially for Rob. Sasha either doesn't see it, or doesn't care.

Truth or Dare. The bottle spins, and points to Nicki.

'The truth is to tell your most embarrassing experience at a party...'

Seems innocent enough. But the bottle is pointing at Nicki. Nothing *that* one does is innocent.

sooz

I suppose you could say she tried to keep it gentle. She told us the most embarrassing thing she'd ever done was get so drunk that she peed on the sofa, and had to blame it on the cat. Everybody was suitably disgusted but laughed along. The game could have just moved on.

But Sasha said, 'That wasn't the most embarrassing thing she did at that party.'

Nicki screamed. 'You dare! You swore.'

She tried to look as though she'd do anything to stop Sasha telling, but we all know her well enough to see she was really enjoying herself.

It turns out that during one of her countless one-night stands, the mindless moron she was trying to get off with dared to suggest that Nicki wasn't lighting his bulb. I could see how much of a challenge that would be for someone like Nicki. Sure enough, she insisted that she could get him going, and asked him what really turned him on.

Girl action. That's what he said.

So Nicki and Sasha snogged in front of him and everyone else who was at the party.

'He couldn't get enough of you after that,' laughed Sasha.

Jamie, predictably, was gagging for more details and probably having trouble controlling the bulge in his trousers.

But Rob... how could Sasha be so casually brutal, so coldly cruel to someone who loves her the way Rob does? His eyes went dead. He wouldn't look at her. And still she didn't stop. I tried to shut her up, but it was like we were all on an unstoppable fairground ride.

'Ooh, what are you scared of, Sooz?' she asked me, in front of everyone. 'Frightened we might find something out about you?'

'Lost your bottle?' Nicki chipped in.

I couldn't bear to give those two the satisfaction of thinking they'd got one over me, so I stayed to watch the next round of humiliation.

The bottle spun again. The dare was to kiss the person on your left. In my case, Jamie. Truth, then.

'Who in this room do you most want to sleep with?'

The bottle pointed at me. Sasha did it on purpose. I know she did. But when I said so, I sounded like a whining nursery school kid.

'I think we've touched a nerve here,' said Nicki.

'Come on, Sooz,' said Sasha. 'Who do you most want to bed?'

Everyone was staring at me. Waiting.

'It's not a difficult question, Sooz.'

SOOZ

Jamie knows, of course. I told him, didn't I, how I feel about Rob? I looked at him and he shook his head slightly. He wasn't going to tell. And then I thought, what the hell? Why don't I just tell them, 'It's Rob, actually. I fancy the pants off Rob.' It would be one in the eye for Sasha, wouldn't it? As for me, I didn't think it could get any more humiliating than it was already, so what did I have to lose?

Sasha (laughing): 'You ever seen Sooz snogging anyone?'

Nicki (laughing): 'Not even any volunteers.'

Alex (laughing): 'Sweet eighteen and never been kissed.'

Sooz (dying): 'Ha ha ha.'

And then I looked at Jamie again, and suddenly he was kissing me. Maybe he sensed I was going to tell, and wanted to shut me up.

I pushed him away and made a big show of disgust. But the thing is...

I don't even want to write it down.

'You look like you enjoyed it to me...'

The thing is, for a moment there, I felt something stirring inside. Something started to turn like an old, disused mill wheel. And I think...

I *think* I started to kiss him back.

SOOZ

There. I've said it. It doesn't feel any better, but it's out.

If things had ended there, it would still have been an unpleasant night, a party I'd rather forget. But it got worse. Sasha and Nicki went on and on with their stupid game. Relentless, no mercy for anyone.

'The dare is, run around the block in your underwear.' Very mature.

'The truth is... who did you lose your virginity to and where?'

The bottle spins. It points to me again. Now I know that Sasha is manipulating it, targeting me. I know I have an amazing ability to make people hate me. But really, what have I ever done to Sasha that makes her want to set me up as a target and shoot non-stop arrows at me?

'We're waiting for Sooz to tell us when she lost her cherry, aren't we, Sooz?'

'You should give it a try, Sooz; it would double your chances of getting a date.'

The bottle was wobbling as if it, too, was waiting. Then Rob said, 'Well, it's gone past Sooz. It's my turn.'

He stood up, and started to take off his shirt. 'How and when and who? Well, that's between me and that person.'

The mood of the party suddenly lifted. We were back to

the kind of Truth or Dare we knew as kids. Rob was about to run round the block in just his underpants.

Nicki said, 'The bottle stopped between both of them. They both have to do the dare.'

I knew she said it to humiliate me just a little bit more, but she doesn't know me as well as she thinks she does. I don't give a toss about people seeing my body. Only what's inside it.

'Doesn't bother me in the slightest,' I said.

Rob and I stripped off, there and then, and started to run round the block. It was genuinely funny – exhilarating, even. Then we turned a corner and almost ran slap-bang into the milkman. We had to dive into the bushes. We were laughing, trying not to make a noise, crushing up against each other so as not to be seen. And then...

Sasha was suspicious when we got back. 'You took your time.'

Rob said, 'Yeah, well, we stopped for breakfast.'

I could feel her eyes on me, even though I had my back to her, getting dressed. But nothing was said.

Sasha and Nicki went too far. It was like they were on another planet somewhere, having a great time, not knowing and maybe not caring about the shower of sparks they were throwing over everyone else. You see, it wasn't just me that got burnt at the Nicki and Sasha grenade-throwing party.

They made Jamie talk about Gabi, and then squealed with laughter whenever he tried to share what it had been like, for him. And then Sasha described, in more detail than you'd ever want to know, her encounter with a virgin who couldn't do it properly.

'When the big moment came, yeah – there was nothing there...'

'Do you know what I said? I took one look at him and I said, "You know what, you're a sexual retard."'

Nicki and Sasha didn't see that they were the only ones laughing. They didn't see Rob squirming like a butterfly caught on a pin, or Alex wriggling on the sofa, or Jamie and me trying to imagine ourselves somewhere, anywhere, other than that room.

And *I'm* the one known as the bitch from hell.

It's not a difficult question.

Something has happened to me. Something huge, radical.

I've started to grow up. How, I couldn't tell you. I think everything that happened with Gabi probably knocked a bit of maturity into me. But I realized how much things have changed last night. When I was with the crowd who have been my best friends for so long, I couldn't remember what life was like before.

I still fancy Nicki, but I'm wondering why. She and Sasha were so cruel to Sooz last night. I haven't seen girls bully one of their own like that since junior school. And Rob, who Sasha claims to love more than anyone in the universe. I watched Rob dying inside. Sasha didn't even realize he was hurting, she just carried on twisting the knife.

jamie

Sasha and Nicki were drunk as skunks. We all were, I suppose. Is that an excuse? It started out as a laugh. We were back at Sasha's house, after a good night at the club. Sasha suggested a game of Truth or Dare, and we were all too far gone to argue. Except Sooz.

She made one of her usual sarky comments, and didn't want to play. Looking back, I think Sooz could see what might happen. Sooz is like granite on the outside, but really she has this amazing sensitive centre. She spots what's going on.

Anyway, the game started.

'The dare is to snog the person on your right...'

In my case, that was Sooz. She gave me a look that said, better tell the truth, boy.

'**... the truth is to tell your most embarrassing experience at a party.**'

Innocent enough. The bottle spins round to Nicki, and Nicki gives us this gross tale about how she wet herself at a party. Then Sasha chips in with an even grosser one about how she and Nicki snogged each other in the club, because Nicki wanted to turn a guy on.

Yeah, it was an exciting thought. It got me going, a bit. Until I looked at Rob's face.

jamie

Sooz could see it too. She tried to stop the game, but Sasha and Nicki were well into it by now. They implied she was too scared to play. That always does it for Sooz. She sat down, and the game carried on.

I don't know if I'm the only one who saw this, but I was watching Sasha's hands on the bottle, and I know for a fact she made it stop at Sooz.

'The dare is to kiss the person on your left...'

'The truth is, who in this room do you most want to sleep with?'

Sooz knew Sasha had cheated, too. I wondered if Sasha suspected how Sooz felt about Rob. They say women have an instinct for stuff like that.

Sooz didn't answer.

'It's not a difficult question, Sooz,' said Sasha impatiently.

'Well, it is if she's trying to name someone who might fancy her back,' laughed Nicki.

So cruel. So unnecessary.

'How do you know?' I said.

Nicki laughed again. 'Oh, is that a confession, Jamie?'

And off they went. Stupid, bitchy remarks about Sooz never having been snogged, stuff like that. And still pressing her to answer. I could see she was tempted to tell them, right there.

Rob, she would say. I want to sleep with Rob.

Suddenly she looked at me. It was the look in her eyes that really got to me. It was like a young deer that's lost its mother, about to be shot, maybe, I dunno. Something awful, scared, pleading. Save me.

So I kissed her. Or she kissed me. Whatever. The dare was to kiss, and we did, so she didn't have to tell the truth. It didn't stop them getting at her – what they said later about her being a virgin was so cruel I can't even write it down. But what's weird, I kissed her because I felt suddenly very protective towards her, more than just being a friend. What's that all about?

I didn't want her to say anything about Rob. Her place in the group is fragile enough, because she's a bit weird. I think everyone would turn on her if she looked like she was trying to break up Rob and Sash. I wanted to save her. And so I kissed her. For longer than a couple of seconds. And she gave me this look...

The game went on. And on. Everybody, except maybe Alex, took their turn as targets for Sasha and Nicki. Even Alex was embarrassed a couple of times.

jamie

It was my turn for the knife when I tried to talk about Gabi.

'Your most intimate moment with a partner.'

I smiled when the bottle stopped at me. I wanted to share what I felt about Gabi, have someone listen and nod, and quietly say, 'Yeah', the way you do when you understand.

Sasha and Nicki were having none of that. Almost as soon as I said her name, they started.

'All you two had was a quick tumble on the South Bank.'

'Did you share a meeting of souls?'

Laughter.

'Did she give you any tips?'

'Yeah, give up.'

More laughter.

We weren't together very long, but that time with Gabi was one of the most important things that ever happened to me. When I found out Gabi was pregnant, later, yeah, I panicked. For about five minutes. Then I realized that I was grown-up enough to take it all on, even Gabi's other kid. When I found out it wasn't mine, I still wanted to do that. I was gutted when she went

jamie

back to her husband. I could have been the one. I would have coped.

But it was just one huge joke to Nicki and Sasha. And I looked at Sooz again, and she put her hand on my arm and gave me this small, sweet smile. She understood, I know she did.

Now, in the cold light of day with a huge hangover, I'm thinking over last night and thinking that maybe we're all at the age when we start to grow up for real, rather than pretending it happened ages ago. And some of us are moving faster than others. Sasha and Nicki? They're back in kindergarten, compared to Sooz and Rob and me. And Alex is probably top junior. I dunno. I just know it's different now. I'm different. We're all still mates, and I still fancy Nicki. But I'm not blind any more.

jamie

Like he was disgusted with me...

The thing with me is, I'm not entirely what you might call balanced. I don't think I'm a complete nutter, but I'm certainly on the bus heading in that direction. I can go from the top of the world to the blackest pit of despair faster than Jamie can scoff down a cheeseburger, and you have to have seen it to believe how fast that is. I can do the journey without any help at all, so when life conspires to take me from heaven to hell in one day, it's a bit much to cope with.

Last night, four of us – Rob, Louise, Jamie and me – had a job at a restaurant. Jamie and the slinky woman in charge have something going on. Quite what is a mystery. I can see why Jamie fancies her – she's an ex-actress, older, gorgeous, has well-placed boobs and bum, and is foreign and exotic. The only quality Jamie looks for in a female is that she's not actually repulsed by him. But what is there about Jamie that a woman like her would want? His vulnerability? That little-boy-lost look, the happy smile that makes you want to smile back, his eagerness to please...? Yes, that's it. Jamie is young, strong, has a penis and will probably do whatever she wants.

Anyway, Jamie and Louise were in the kitchen, Rob and I were waiting at tables. I wore a short black skirt and white top, with my hair tied back, like you have to when you're a waitress. I could see that Rob liked the look of me. He came closer, and smiled.

'You smell nice,' he said.

My stomach lurched. He was so close. I wanted to reach out and touch his face. I didn't, of course. Apart from anything else, I had two plates of dinner in my hands.

All evening I had this weird feeling that Rob was looking at me. He dropped soup on a customer – not concentrating because he was smiling at me. And I dropped two plates because I was laughing at his impression of a French wine waiter.

The sexy piece didn't fancy me and Rob as much as Jamie, obviously. She gave us the sack. I think that's what 'Get out!' means.

SOOZ

Poor Jamie. He was upset for us, wanted to sort it out. Ever the peacemaker, eh, Jamie? But not this time. Rob was my knight in shining armour.

'Don't worry, Jamie,' I said. 'I'm leaving. You can stay here and get treated like a dog.'

The French bitch said something like, 'I treat people as I find them.'

Rob said, 'Don't talk to her like that.' Just like he would say if it was Sasha.

I was up in the clouds. Rob was defending my honour. Protecting me, like a boyfriend would.

'I asked you for someone who was human, Jamie,' she said, looking at me as though I'd been dragged in by one of the cats they serve up in their chicken dishes.

Rob got very manly then. 'You say one more word about her...' He sounded quite threatening. 'Come on.'

He took my hand – he took my hand! – and we walked away. We found an empty function room, and Rob opened a bottle of champagne he'd lifted from the kitchen. I doubt we'll get any pay, so it seemed fair enough. We danced the tango, we drank, we sat on the sofa and talked. We...

We kissed. We kissed for a long time. And although he said sorry, because it was a bit like kissing a sister, he kissed me again. And I know, without any shadow of a doubt, that it would have gone further if Jamie hadn't burst through the door at that moment and seen us. I wanted it to go further. More importantly, so did Rob.

He was upset by Jamie coming in. It spoiled everything, because Rob stopped and took me home. We kissed again there, even though I could see he was worried about what Jamie would do. And he was very quiet.

I didn't care who knew. I was worried for Jamie, because I knew he'd be upset and confused. But what the hell, tell the world, I thought. Finally, Sooz can prove once and for all that it's not true no man would want to go near her, even for a bet. The most gorgeous man in the world is at her side, wanting her.

That was heaven. I lay awake all night wondering what would happen, how Rob would tell Sasha he was with me now, whether the gang would blame me, whether Sasha would hit me as well as Rob when she knew. All kinds of stuff was running through my head. I tried to call Rob, but he didn't answer. Then I tried again and he said he couldn't talk because he was at Sasha's house.

That was the early indication that I was about to slide down from my little cloud. My first thought was that maybe he was telling her. But my sensible head said no, he was probably back with her. I told myself how real the kiss was, how much I loved him and would fight for him. How bad Sasha was for him and how he must, finally, see that for himself.

But the little demon on my shoulder kept saying, 'Why would someone like Rob want you? No man would take you, even for a bet. Eighteen and still a virgin. What does that tell you? It was the drink, stupid. Get real.'

Still, the next day, when I saw Rob in the café, I was hopeful. I smiled at him. He looked away. He brought coffee, I spilled it, our hands touched, he pulled away. Like he was disgusted with me, with what we'd done.

It was my mistake.

He didn't even want to look at me. But he and Sasha... I sat watching them, kissing and cuddling and laughing together. Like last night had never happened. Like I was nothing, the kiss with me was nothing. So why did he kiss me back, why did he run his hands over my body, why did he...

If Jamie hadn't come in when he did, there would have been no turning back. And now, it's like I was part of a bad dream. He wants to blot me out.

Jamie came up beside me. 'Sooz...'

I knew he felt bad for me. But sympathy of any sort was

more than I could take. I was breaking apart. One kind word would have thrown me on the rocks. So I ran for it. No one noticed, of course – except, perhaps, Jamie. That's how important I am.

I sat in the loos and sobbed like a little kid. Real hard, I am. That's what they think, that's what I give them. I cried, I mopped up the tears, I pulled myself together, replaced the armour and went back.

But it wasn't over yet. When I went back in, there was a strange sort of bubbly excitement in the air. Jamie looked absolutely miserable but all the others were grinning like idiots at an idiot party.

'Hey Sooz,' shouted Alex. 'Sash and Rob are moving in together!'

I felt Jamie's hand slip into mine. Quietly, not noticed by anyone. He knew the ground was falling away underneath me. I was losing it, big time.

I felt my lips move around the word, but it was a while before I could get the sound out. 'Congratulations,' I said finally. 'I'm really pleased for you.'

I went outside and sat on the bench. What else can you do when there is no hope, no joy, no purpose in life? Getting to the bench was as much as I could manage.

I'll just sit here all alone until I grow old and shrivelled, I thought. Then I'll die, and someone will come and sweep me up with the rest of the rubbish. And that will be that.

Jamie came and sat by me. 'He's always had dodgy taste in women,' he said.

I tried to smile. I knew Jamie was hurting for me and wanted to make it better. Why can't I love Jamie, who's available, instead of Rob, who isn't? It's a cruel design feature that's built in to humans so that their miserable, failing little lives can amuse the gods. We're all just acting out a huge soap opera, a kind of divine *EastEnders*. And the mysterious forces out there, whatever they are, sit slobbing on a sofa discussing our little lives and predicting what will happen in the next episode. Except that they know already, of course.

Jamie was still trying. 'It's a nice dress,' he said.

'Shut up, will you?' I said. But he was smiling at me. You have to smile back at Jamie, you can't help it. Even when you're trying very hard not to cry.

'Come on. Mmm? The mushy peas are on me.' Gently, Jamie took my arm and pulled me up.

Why can't I fancy Jamie, instead of wasting my life pining for Rob?

Our Sooz, in the prettiest pink outfit...

14, Hereward House, Tooting, South London

Monday

Dear Mum,

Just a quick note to say thanks for the lovely flowers and chocolates. It was a great birthday, and even better because you were able to stay over. I hope the train wasn't too crowded on the way back.

I enclose a photo of our Sooz. Doesn't she look sweet? They're not her clothes, they're a friend's. Sooz says she had to wear them because she got locked out while I was off at the shops. She had to borrow something or freeze, she says. But really, I think she's turning a corner. Not before time, I know. She made a big thing of ripping everything off as soon as she got through the door, but secretly she wants to be a proper feminine woman. I'm going to see what I can get her for Christmas from that new boutique on the High Street, to help her along.

Bill and Gary are both doing well and send their love. As does Sooz, in her own way (snarling from the corner)!

Talk to you soon,

Love,

Marianne

14, Hereward House

Tooting

South London

Monday

Dear Ruth,

Look at this! Yes, it's our Sooz in the prettiest pink outfit you could hope for. Doesn't she look great? I knew you'd be as pleased as me, and relieved as well, to find that your niece was finally making an effort to be normal.

I put Mum on the train yesterday, thank God. You ought to know that although I wanted to kill her at least seven times over the weekend, I stayed calm and didn't touch her once. But it's your turn, come Christmas, so be warned.

Love,

Marianne

Tedious Tooting   *Yesterday*

Dear Em,

I expect by now you've seen it. The vision-nightmare, in pink, that Mum seems to be sending all around the family. If we're gonna stay cousins and good friends, you are going to have to get it back for me, or else I might have to leave the country.

I got locked out of the flat wearing very little, see. (No, take your mind out of the gutter, I was just sitting on the stairs, reading). Mum was off on one of her shopping binges. And the only friend I could get to answer my mayday call was Nicki. You know, the slapper. She saw me as a bit of a challenge and dressed me up like a Barbie doll. It was the ultimate nightmare experience. People from college saw me, the gang at the coffee shop had a great laugh, and finally Mum swooped in with a camera. She actually went and borrowed it on her way home, so she could get a piccy before I got inside the house and took them off. How sad is that?

You gotta help me, Em, just like I helped you over that thing with Dean. And while you're at it, next time you're round at Nan's and she's off on one of her daydreams, can you swipe the photo Mum sent to her as well? God knows how many copies she's had made, but I can at least do a bit of damage limitation. Cheers, Em.

My love life is as sad as ever. How goes it with Col?

Love,

SOOZ

...she **was** going to jump.

I could murder Sooz. If I didn't have a sneaky feeling she would be willing to do the job herself.

That train thing scared me more than I've ever been scared in my whole life. I knew she was down, because of Rob and Sasha being back together. And I know Rob asked her to tell Sasha nothing happened, even though it did. He was a bastard to her, but the fact is he still loves Sasha and Sooz was a mistake. I don't suppose it feels very good to be told that by someone you love – that you're just a mistake.

She tried to push it by 'accidentally' saying something to me about her and Rob kissing, when she knew full well Sasha was listening. There was a huge row, and Sasha

jamie

walked out. I think Sooz thought she had a chance then, but Rob made it clear she didn't.

'Look, I don't fancy you, Sooz. It's not going to happen, all right?'

I had tried to warn her. I mean, Rob talks to me, doesn't he? So if there was any chance, I would know. I didn't want to tell Sooz what he had said, about her or about Sasha. But I knew she wasn't in the running, not even close. She wouldn't listen.

Later, back at her house, I tried to get her to talk. She was doing her usual prickly pear routine, when I found a poem she'd written tucked into a book by the bed.

Lips. Mouth. Tasted so sweet.
Fire. Passion. Finally we meet.

'Oh, I never knew you had it in you,' I said. 'This is so girlie, Sooz.'

It was meant to be a joke. I wasn't trying to hurt her. But she went completely ape.

'You're so sick!' she said, and kicked me. Hard.

I said, 'Oh, excuse me for breathing.'

And she said, 'No, Jamie, excuse me for living.'

jamie

It was a weird thing to say, but then Sooz is a weird woman. She stormed out with a look about her that I've never seen before. It was more than angry, it was kind of... I couldn't put my finger on it.

I assumed she'd be back after a couple of minutes. She usually is, ready to pretend nothing has happened which is her kind of apology when she knows she's overreacted. But she didn't come back. I leafed through her books, found some more poetry and some other things she's written down about what's going on inside her head.

That was when I understood the look on her face when she stormed out. Desperate. Without hope.

'Excuse me for living.'

A knot of fear started growing in my belly. I ran like a madman, ran round all the usual places. No sign. So I went to the Tube station. Sometimes, when I'm really hacked off, I just go for a long ride to nowhere. It gives me space to think and get my head together. I thought maybe Sooz would do the same.

From the tunnel, you can see the whole station. She

jamie

was there, right on the very edge of the platform. A train was moving in.

Right on the very edge, with her head down. She swayed slightly. Her eyes were closed. She was going to jump.

I yelled something, don't know what, it sounded like an animal in a trap. And I ran. I screamed out her name, over and over, sometimes in my head, sometimes aloud.

When I reached the platform, there was no sign of her. I was hot, and great globs of sweat were rolling down my face. Suddenly there were tears there as well.

'Jamie, what are you doing here?'

I turned around, and there was Sooz. I hugged her, and she pushed me off.

She says she had no intention of jumping.

'You're such a drama queen... Do you really think I hate life that much?'

Yes. Yes, I do think she hates life that much. And whatever she says, I know she *was* going to jump. I hope to God whatever stopped her jumping stays with her, because I couldn't bear not having her around. As a friend, that's all.

jamie

She's frightened me, now. I don't understand what makes her tick. I think I do, and then something like this happens. It makes me scared, and angry, and it makes me want to kill her. Which is totally nuts. So maybe we are suited after all.

She's a better fighter than you'd think, to look at her.

I was not going to jump.

I'm not denying that it came close.

Sometimes I feel like I'm drowning in a huge, black pit of heaving slime. It comes from nowhere, and it's impossible to describe properly. The closest to it is what I saw in a film once – *The Man in the Iron Mask*.

Leonardo DiCaprio (I fancied him in those days, but don't hold it against me) played a prince who had a twin brother. When they were born, their father was worried that they might fight over the crown when they got older. So he pretended there was only one baby, and had one taken away. When the boy was a bit older, they put him in an iron mask so no one could see his face, and imprisoned him a deep, dark pit so he could never get out.

SOOZ

When I saw him in the pit I gasped. I almost cried out. I knew, exactly, what that felt like. It was me, the darker twin of *me*. The only way I can fight it is to release the bitch from hell, as Jamie so lovingly calls me. The bigger the act, the bigger the chance of holding off the despair. Then it comes crashing down, and I fall into the pit anyway.

You're thinking I need help, right? I do. But not yet. One day, maybe, before I fall in the pit for the last time and can't get out.

I wasn't going to jump. All right, it crossed my mind, but only for a moment.

Jamie's been treating me like a tragic case ever since. He looks at me with troubled eyes, and says, 'All right, Sooz?' And he follows me about, or phones to ask what I'm doing. It's driving me nuts.

It's not as though he's exactly centred, is it? I mean – he fancies Nicki, even though everyone knows she's a slapper who'll use anybody and anything to get what she wants.

Last night, she asked Jamie to take her to the party we were throwing for Louise. He was like a puppy with a new bone.

'I get to go to Nicki's house, take her for a drink, take her to the party.'

SOOZ

I wondered what the hell Nicki was up to. I know she thinks Jamie is cute, but he's not in her league, usually. He was bound to get hurt.

I reminded him he was supposed to be helping me get the party ready.

'Oh Sooz, we're mates, yeah, but you do realize you don't get a look in here...'

Just as well I'm not suicidal, then, isn't it? If I am going to jump – which I'm not, but if I were – better make it a day when Nicki's fully occupied or no one will even notice I've gone.

I knew Nicki was up to something and sure enough, at the party I could see she was using Jamie to try and make Chris jealous. Chris is the kind of bloke who'll sleep with anything in a skirt. He's a walking sleaze bucket. All roads lead to some kind of sexual destination as far as he's concerned. Right up Nicki's street, actually.

Who would believe that Jamie could make someone like Chris jealous? Incredible, eh? But when I was in the loo, I heard Nicki telling Sash that Jamie was her 'Plan B', if she couldn't get Chris. Meanwhile, poor old Jamie's out there in the bar, drooling in anticipation of a night to remember with the girl of his dreams.

SOOZ

I couldn't bear it. I flew out of the loo and grabbed Nicki's arm.

'Don't play with Jamie,' I said.

'Oh – nice little eavesdrop?' Nicki laughed. She didn't care that I had caught her out.

'You know he likes you, so why do you have to mess him around?'

'If you fancy him, just tell me and I'll back off,' she said.

'I don't fancy him!'

'Then why are you so bothered? It's not me you're interested in, is it?'

'Don't flatter yourself,' I said, disgusted.

'Don't worry, Sooz, I won't tell anyone,' she laughed, and kissed me. There was lipstick all over my face. Bitch.

'Mustn't keep Jamie waiting...'

She sloped off, wiggling her bum and looking back over her shoulder at me. She knew she looked absolutely gorgeous, and Jamie was going to be in seventh heaven for every second that he thought he had a chance with her.

I watched them start to dance. When Chris looked over, Nicki started snogging Jamie like there was no tomorrow. Jamie thought this was his moment, and gave it all he had.

I went up to them and stood in the middle. I insisted that I had to talk to Jamie, right there and then.

Nicki said to Jamie, 'Come and find me when you get your mother off your back,' and disappeared.

Jamie was furious. I tried to explain.

'She's using you to get at Chris,' I said. 'You're just "Plan B".'

'I don't care if I'm the "Break glass in case of emergency" plan. I just had Nicki – repeat, Nicki – pressed up against me.'

I couldn't believe what I was hearing. 'Do you have any pride?' I asked.

'Where she's concerned, no,' he said.

Then he moved me out of his way and went off to find Nicki. But by then, of course, she was making a move on Chris. They more or less ignored Jamie and went off together.

So I was proved right. But Jamie was still mad with me. Not with Nicki, who had strung him along and then gone off with another man, but with me, the friend who tried to save him. How fair is that?

'She was making a fool of you,' I protested.

'Not before you butted in.'

'I was thinking of you, Jamie,' I said.

'No, you weren't.'

He stomped off, and wouldn't talk to me.

Now I happen to know – and don't ask me how because I'm

too embarrassed to tell — that Chris and Nicki had it off in the stock room at the back of the club. I also know that he'd given her the brush-off as soon as they'd finished, and she was a bit narked by that. Well, it must be galling to be treated like a disposable accessory when you've been the one doing that to people all your life. She looked close to tears, but it was a bit much to expect sympathy from me.

She recovered quite quickly, though, because next minute she was all over Jamie. I was so mad, I tried to pull them apart.

'You have got no morals,' I shouted at her, but she didn't care.

Jamie said, 'Shut it, Sooz, you've got this all wrong.'

'She's just had sex with Chris,' I said.

Jamie looked shell-shocked, but Nicki was annoyed, nothing more.

'Oh, tell the world, why don't you,' she said.

'You're such a little slapper,' I said.

Actually, I shouted. I could feel something about to snap.

'*And you are just a twisted little virgin who hates the thought of anyone else having any fun.*'

That's when the fight started. She's a better fighter than you'd think, to look at her. She fights dirty, too. But not as dirty as me. I blackened her eye, and I'm not sorry.

SOOZ

Jamie has no dignity at all. He didn't see through Nicki even then.

'Well done, Sooz. Not only have you ruined my night, but everyone else's as well... All you've done is make a pranny of yourself.'

'I was trying to do you a favour,' I said.

'Well, try getting some help,' Jamie said.

It was on the tip of my tongue to tell him I had decided to do just that, and to ask him to come with me. You know, sit in the canteen so I've got someone's arm to hold on to once I've lain on the couch and spilled the beans. But he looked so angry.

'I'm sick of listening to you and your hang-ups and your stupid schoolgirl crushes. Find someone else.'

'... I'm your friend,' I said. I could feel tears welling up, so I put my vicious expression on, to try and stop them.

'And what exactly do I get from this friendship? Constant put-downs and your ugly beak in my business. I just don't want it any more.'

He turned and walked away. Just like that. He's never done that before. I've never seen him angry like this. He must really feel something for Nicki. And, as usual, I've spoiled everything.

SOOZ

I left the club. It felt like I was walking to the edge of the pit again. I found myself at the station, just like before.

No, I wasn't going to jump. I don't think so, anyway. It's just that standing there on the edge of the platform, with the train's lights winking in the gloom, you start to think. The rhythm of the train, and the sound as it gets closer, feels like an invitation.

One second and it will all be over. You won't feel anything. Oblivion. Eternal peace. You'll never have to speak, or think, or feel again. One moment of courage, one jump, that's all it takes.

Yeah, I need help.

SOUTH LONDON NHS TRUST: LIFELINK
ST ANSELM'S HOSPITAL, TRUDING ROAD, LONDON SE12
TEL. 0207 981 76662 FAX. 0207 981 76673

Miss Suzanne Lee
14, Hereward House,
Tooting,
London
SW17 4BJ   date as postmark

Dear Miss Lee,

Following your consultation with your GP, an appointment has
been made for you at our 'LifeLink' clinic on

    Wednesday 21 November.

    At this initial consultation you will be seen by

    Dr Miriam Shultz

    Part of this first consultation will be used to decide how
many sessions with us you are likely to need, and when these will
be. You will need to bring your diary, or a note of any dates you
will not be able to make within the next three months, to the consultation.

    If you are unable to come on the date specified above, please
contact us as soon as possible so that a new date can be arranged.

    A leaflet explaining something of the work of the clinic is
enclosed for your information.

    Yours sincerely,

M. Wildman
Appointments Clerk

LifeLink Clinic

You have been referred to us by your doctor because s/he believes you will benefit from talking through your problems with someone skilled in helping people who are in distress. You and the doctor at the clinic will decide how many times, and how frequently, you will need to come to us. We cannot promise easy answers, and you will have to work as hard as we do to find your way through the despair, but together we believe we stand the best chance of recovering your wellbeing.

Our clients usually come for six to eight sessions of one hour in length, but this is not always the case. You and the doctor will decide together what is best. You will be encouraged to come on the same day at a regular time, to establish a routine. So before you come, give some thought to the day that will suit you best.

LifeLink Clinic rarely prescribes drugs, but if the doctor feels you need anti-depressants or any other kind of medication, this will be thoroughly discussed with you. Your GP will prescribe any medicine needed and supervise this part of your care.

Many people find the idea of talking over their problems daunting, even frightening at first. Everyone you meet at the clinic understands these fears, but emotional or mental illness, just like a broken arm or a stubborn virus, can respond to treatment and you can get back to excellent health again.

You will be asked to do a lot of talking and sometimes this will be about things that you would rather not face. LifeLink Clinic cannot promise that it will be easy, but if you are committed to sorting out the things that are troubling you and making you unwell, we are here for you.

SOUTH LONDON NHS TRUST

LifeLink Clinic

working for your wellbeing

St Anselm's Hospital,
Truding Road, London, SE12

Tel: 0207 981 76662
Fax: 0207 981 76673

The truth is, I was a prat.

At the time, it seemed like one of my best ideas ever. You'd think I would have learned by now that when it comes to my ideas, things go wrong in direct proportion to how good I thought the idea was.

Mum was going on about her Reader's Digest prize draw and how she couldn't believe she had been 'specially selected'. All the same, she couldn't resist filling in the little form, just in case...

It gave me an idea. I made cards with my name and number on, and I gave them out. I gave one to any girl I liked the look of. So if any one of them replied – and statistically, I reckoned on about 2 to 5 per cent or four to ten girls – the expense would have been worth it, right? The beauty of the plan was, I was in control of who got a

jamie

card and who didn't. So if a girl was a minger, or too old, or too skinny or whatever, she didn't get a card. Therefore I knew that whoever phoned me back was going to be someone attractive and sexy. Couldn't lose.

I still have faith in the system. I just made a dud choice. Lilli looked good, smelled good, seemed to feel the same way about me. Liar, liar. She was already spoken for – just a bit bored, I guess. And when she suggested a party, I wasn't exactly reluctant.

Lilli must have thought I was a right plonker, providing a party for her and her mates without any complaint. When it all went wrong, she just shrugged her shoulders and left me to cope with the fallout. And Sasha dishes fallout like no other woman on earth.

I admit I deserved it. I persuaded Sasha and Rob to throw a party in a borrowed flat they were being trusted to look after. I begged Sooz to borrow her brother's decks for me and promised to guard them with my life. I even ate a tomato, though I'm allergic to tomatoes and knew I would throw up, just to amuse Sooz and make her lend me the decks.

The truth is, I was a prat. I fell for Lilli's flirty little smiles without seeing the huge great boyfriend and the thugs

jamie

she had in tow. I misread all the signs and ended up being responsible for the fight. Sooz says that bit wasn't my fault – Nicki started the fight. But if I hadn't let Lilli string me along it wouldn't have happened, would it? So it's down to me.

Sasha and Rob were shattered. Luckily everyone at my place is away for the weekend – Dad's friend from work is getting married. So I gave them my keys, sent them back to my place and promised to put the flat straight and have all the damage repaired.

When they'd left, and I was sitting there with my rubber gloves trying to work out where to start, and how I was going to afford to replace all the broken stuff, I got to thinking.

Is this it? Is this going to be my life? One stupid adolescent crisis after another? Mine or someone else's, it's all the same. My life's not making sense, there's something missing. There's no direction, no sense of achievement, no ambition. And no one to share with, either. I'm eighteen years old. An adult. I can fight in a war, vote, get married. The law says I'm a grown man, and I can do anything a grown man can do. So how come I feel like a Year Nine kid?

jamie

REPAIRS LIST

Buy: 2 wine glasses, round ones

1 beer mug

deck repairs (look in *Yellow Pages*)

carpet shampoo

stain remover for sofa

rawl plugs and screws to repair curtain rail (ask Dad)

laundry — bed cover (ask Mum about beer stains) and
   towels (soak first to get vomit off)

curtains — dry clean?

French polish/scratch repair for table (ask Dad)

garbage sacks

rubber gloves

new window for cracked one in hall (*Yellow Pages*)

flowers and a bottle for Sash and Rob

heart-shaped chocs from corner shop

jamie

I was feeling really down, and that's unusual for me. I knew I had to put the flat back to rights – it was the least I could do for Sash and Rob. So I got started sweeping up the broken glass and stuff.

My gran always used to say that when you're down in the gutter it might be the only chance you get to look up and see the stars. That always seemed stupid to me. I didn't understand it. Nor did I understand what the teacher in English GCSE was going on about when she said something was ironic.

Both those concepts make perfect sense to me now. I was about as down as I'm capable of being that night. I just wanted to get through to the morning, put the flat right and get out of there.

And then Sooz arrived. No fuss, she was suddenly just there, helping out. She didn't do a huge song and dance routine about how irresponsible I was, or how I only had myself to blame (though both those things were true). She knew I was in the gutter, and she quietly came along and picked me up. It was like Gran was saying, Come on, look at the stars, boy.

Irony? All this time I've been longing for Someone. I've chased all sorts of women in all sorts of stupid ways.

jamie

I've roamed the whole world – on the Internet, at least – looking for the right person. And all the time that Someone was right under my nose.

Sooz. She's weird, but so am I. She gets incredibly down, and I don't understand that sort of stuff. But I can be happy for both of us if I have to. She's sweet and sensitive and funny and she accepts me the way I am. We're two halves of the same apple, as my gran would say.

We talked, properly, for maybe the first time ever. She told me that she *had* meant to jump, the night I saw her at the station. I was shocked. Then I knew that I couldn't bear not to have her around: wheeling me about in a nicked supermarket trolley, clipping me round the ear, making me eat tomatoes to punish me, snarling like a little tiger cub when she thinks I'm being naff.

I think I might fancy Sooz. That's the truth. I certainly want to kiss her again.

Oh yeah, didn't I mention that? We kissed.

jamie

It's not as though Jamie is anything to me.

Jamie really lost it over that thing with Nicki. I thought when he calmed down a bit he would understand I was only looking out for him, being a good friend. But days later he was still furious. He avoided me; I watched him scuttle away whenever he saw me coming. It hurt.

Then I did see him, in the café, dishing out little cards. Straight up, he was handing out business cards – *Jamie Collier 079977106511773 Call me!* – to just about any woman he saw. Not me, of course. I had to find out from someone else what was going on. Refuge of the desperate, or what? (Him, I mean, handing out cards to strange women. Not me, asking a strange woman what her card said.)

I don't know why I cared. It's not as though Jamie is anything to me. If he wants to make a fool of himself, why should

I stop him? And yet, I stuck my beak in. Why? Search me. Protective instinct, maybe.

He hooked up with the gorgeous Lilli. You could see she was stringing him along a mile off. Why else would a girl like that respond to a sad git like Jamie handing out cards? Lilli implied Jamie would be on to a winner if he threw a party, so he persuaded Sash and Rob to have a 'housewarming' party at the flat – which isn't even theirs. Rob could see problems with it, but Sash lives only for the moment and only for herself. So the party was arranged.

'I just think you use people,' I said to Jamie later. 'Have you even told Rob and Sasha why you're so keen on them having this party?'

He looked at me and turned away, humming a tune to show he wasn't listening, like a little kid. Fair enough, I thought, let him get hurt. Why should I bother? So I left, but he chased after me.

He said, 'Once upon a time, you weren't getting any, you weren't bitter. Everyone knew where they stood. Now, you're trying to stop everyone else getting any under any circumstances. You need help.'

That was cruel. He knows it's a sore spot with me, being a virgin. And don't I know I need help?

'Do you know what I need, Jamie?' I said. 'I need some decent friends.'

'Yeah, well try acting like a decent human being for a change!'

If I had a quid for every time someone has made reference to me as sub-human, I'd be bathing in champagne and living in a penthouse suite. How did I manage to go from concerned friend to inhuman ragbag? I wish I knew, 'cos it seems to happen a lot. It's got to be me – something wrong with me. Hasn't it?

Later on, Jamie changed his tune because he wanted to borrow my brother's decks. He'd told the gorgeous Lilli that he was a nifty DJ. Roll over, Fatboy Slim. Suddenly I was good old Sooz again, as if he'd done nothing to hurt and humiliate me.

The lying sleazebag pitched in with, 'I've been meaning to say... about you stopping Nicki the other night... I know that in your mind it was a good thing to do. And I'm sorry about the stuff I said about you having mental problems.'

He must have been desperate. He bought me snacks, followed me around, even grovelled and offered to lick my shoes. Disgusting. (Actually, I should have made him, 'cos I'd walked through the park and there was dog pooh on one of them. That would have taught him.)

He begged and begged.

'Please Sooz, I'm desperate. Anything you want me to do, I'll do, but you've got to get me that deck.'

Rash, Jamie my friend, rash. There was something repellent about him begging and pleading like that, just so he could impress a girl he'd picked up off the street and didn't know from Eve. I felt angry because he thought he could just get away with it. It was anger, you see. Not jealousy.

So I made him eat a tomato. Jamie can get about halfway through a tomato before he throws up in a big way. He has a splitting headache for hours afterwards too. So I figured if he was prepared to eat a tomato to get his hands on those decks, maybe he really did have feelings for this Lilli person.

He ate it. Well, half of it. I let him off the rest. I couldn't bear to hear him vomiting any more.

The party was good for about half an hour. Then Lilli arrived. Her boyfriend came too, plus some other gatecrashers. I can't believe Jamie didn't see what was going on. The blokes went into the kitchen and started on the booze straight away. Jamie was falling over himself to get it together with Lilli; he didn't have eyes for anything or anyone else.

Then Nicki got it into her head that Alex and Chris had a thing going. I don't know which dark recesses of the empty

SOOZ

space inside her head she dragged that idea from, but I can see why she might be galled by it. Chris had been groping her bum and talking dirty into her ear only two minutes before she saw him with Alex.

It was an amusing little scene, when she confronted them. Chris didn't have the faintest idea what she was going on about. Alex guessed. He knows Nicki so well.

He said, 'You know, Nicki – the difference between you and me is that I can actually talk to a bloke and not want to get into his trousers.'

I laughed. Nicki came stalking over to me, in a right huff.

'What are you looking at?'

'Oh, I just find it amusing, that's all. You know, Chris isn't interested in you, so he's got to be gay.' And I laughed again.

That's when the fight started. Jamie got the blame, but it was Nicki's fault. All right, Nicki's and mine. We started rowing. Nicki pushed me and I went to hit her. Alex, remembering the last fight we had, stepped between us and Nicki pushed him out of the way. He fell against someone who elbowed him in the face and... the rest, as they say, is history. Meanwhile, Jamie came to blows with the huge bloke who everyone except Jamie had guessed was Lilli's man, and had to make a run for it.

Sasha finally threw a wobbly and stopped the party. Wise move. It was pretty well trashed, the flat. She and Rob were furious. And somehow Jamie was taking the rap.

He looked crushed, old, tired, I don't know what. Something about him, standing there taking it, made me feel sorry for him even though I'd been ready to kill him a couple of minutes before. I can't get my feelings straight about Jamie at the moment. My mouth opens and words come out without anything happening to my brain in between.

Jamie persuaded Rob and Sasha to go back to his place for the night while he stayed to clean up. Back home, I had to call him. I couldn't get his sweet, sad expression and deeply crushed look out of my head.

His voice was flat. I recognized that tone. I hear it in my own voice often enough on bad days. So I went back to the flat to help him out.

He hugged me, told me he was a prat (I wasn't going to disagree there). Then we cleaned up. It was a laugh, like the old days when we did stuff together. Made me realize how sour and serious everything has been lately. Me and Rob, Jamie and Gabi, Alex and Dan. Even Rob and Sasha. No one seems happy.

Tired out, we slumped on the sofa with a mug of tea and

SOOZ

surveyed the clean flat with pride. We made a list of stuff left to do, and stuff Jamie would have to buy. Then we just lay there, recovering. We were so tired and so full of drink that the little game we fell into – Mr and Mrs Happy Couple of Happy-Happy Land – seemed very entertaining to us.

'Can I have a biccie, darling?' I asked.

'Help yourself, darling,' he said.

And so on. We pretended to adore each other. We even pretended to kiss. But only pretended. We were drunk.

When we'd sobered up a bit, we carried the deck back to my place. We needed to get Jamie in and out of the flat before my brother discovered what had happened, or he may not have got out of there alive.

We stopped for a rest on a bench, and sat silent for a while, looking out over the park. I thought about how Jamie had looked the night before, and how something inside me had pulled tight, seeing him like that.

I'm a prat.

I said, 'OK, so you're a prat... but at least you're out there, doing it. Making mistakes. I just stay at home being bitter.'

'No you don't.'

'Yeah, OK, you're right. I'm also capable of going out and being bitter.'

We laughed. But there was a strange feeling in the air: warm, mellow, comfy, like it hasn't been between us for ages.

'You don't make it easy for yourself, you know,' Jamie said. 'I mean sometimes... for people to like you.'

My heart started to thump. It was getting a bit personal, close to home. I trotted out one of my usual flippant throw-aways. 'We can't all be Mr Charm, you know.'

But I could see that Jamie was trying to say something important. My heart started to go even faster. 'Sorry,' I said. 'If you really want to know, I'm not exactly my own favourite person most of the time either.'

'Sooz, I know you've been down and that recently. All the Rob stuff — him and Sasha moving in and... I know it can't have been easy for you.'

Jamie has no idea just how down I can get. His tenderness made me want to cry.

'I'm all right,' I said, trying to look away.

'Yeah, you're all right, but...' His hand was in mine and my heart was revving up for take-off so loud I bet he could hear it. 'We used to have more of a laugh, though...'

'I haven't felt much like laughing recently,' I said.

SOOZ

I told him. I don't know why. I've never talked about my feelings with anyone before. Maybe I knew it would be easier with him than with a therapist who was a complete stranger, maybe it was because he made it so easy. Whatever it was, I told him that he'd been right, that day, at the train station.

'Bloody hell, Sooz.'

'It's all right. I didn't do it, did I?'

'You can't go around doing that sort of thing.' He had his arms around me now. It felt good, warm, safe. It felt like I belonged there, on that bench with Jamie's arms around me. It's such a long time since I've felt like I belong anywhere.

'Never knew you cared,' I said.

The next thing... Jamie kissed me. And I kissed him back.

Now I'm in the pit again. I've spoiled it all. Everything will go sour, it always does. And Jamie is the best friend I've ever had. That stupid kiss, if we're not careful, will make us 'an item', as Nicki would say. For a while, we'll be happy together. But the time will come to pay the price. He'll find out how screwed up I really am, and he'll dump me. I'll have nobody.

I am so scared. My feelings are getting out of control, and I can't stop them.

I wish that kiss had never happened.

SOOZ

I'll end up wearing a collar and chain.

I can't take much more of this. We kissed, it meant something, I know it did. I dream about her (funnily enough, she's quite normal in my dreams, wears skirts and high heels and everything) and I wake up thinking, yeah.

So why is Sooz blowing hot and cold all the time? One minute she's down my tonsils, the next she's behaving like I took advantage, and she's not interested.

'We might've exchanged saliva – but it doesn't give you a say in my social life, OK?'

'You have no claims on me, Jamie, comprende?'

It's like she has to fight to get turned on. We argue, we chase each other around, we grab hold of each other...

jamie

she's not the only one turned on by it, actually. But I don't want it to be that kind of deal, not as a regular thing. I'll end up wearing a collar and chain, and her making me eat dog doo or something. I want to do it with Sooz – I badly want to do it with Sooz, but I think we should be about more than kinky sex. I know I sound like my dad, but I can't help it.

Then suddenly, she'll go all soft and sweet, like a Sooz I've never known before, and... and I fancy her.

'You're not my boyfriend, OK?'

That got me. Right, I thought, if you want to play that little game, I'm in. So I went on the pull, and scored. Honestly, women are like buses... no, all right, that's an old one. Anyway, I met this cool dude of a woman, Anna. She was keen, we got on really well. Sooz didn't like that at all. Serve her right, I thought. At first, I only wanted to flirt with Anna to make Sooz a bit jealous, but Sooz behaved like a cow, so I took it a bit further. Hands up, I was wrong. But I was provoked.

Anyway, Sooz saw me going off with Anna at the end of the evening. She also saw us first thing next morning,

jamie

in the café. Two and two make four, right? Obviously we'd slept together. Sooz stormed off.

Only we hadn't. Anna wanted to, but I couldn't. I want Sooz. It would just have been using Anna and hurting Sooz. I couldn't do it.

I ran after Sooz, to explain. I expected another row, a fight maybe, and I knew where a fight might lead... but no. Sooz was uncharacteristically reasonable, friendly even. She didn't want to listen to an explanation, but she wasn't going to fight either.

'I mean, hopefully it's not impossible for us to be adults about this, is it?'

Luckily she found out from what the others were saying that I hadn't done anything with Anna. Rob heard me telling Anna there was someone else. Naturally, everyone wanted to know who that someone was. I think I might even have told them, if it wasn't for Alex. He burst in on Sooz and me while we were... talking, and went back to the others to announce that we were an item. As a joke.

It was awful. Everyone started laughing.

jamie

Alex said, 'Sorry, mate. I told them about that dream you had – when you and Sooz were a couple.'

'Nightmare, more like,' I said. I could have kicked myself in the balls straight away when I saw Sooz's face. I said it because I was embarrassed, and because I was used to being a lad, and I forgot what was going on.

'So who is she, Jamie? Who is your secret girlfriend?'

'Is it Gabi?'

Now was the time. I looked at Sooz. I was going to tell them. I took a nervous breath...

'A woman with two heads couldn't be that desperate,' said Sooz quickly.

Everyone laughed.

'A desperate woman with two heads and a week to live couldn't be that desperate!'

They laughed again, and she looked at me until I looked away.

'There is no girlfriend,' I said. 'All right? If I had a girl-friend, you'd all be the first to know.'

I looked at Sooz, ready to stare her out this time, but she was looking out of the window and I couldn't see her face.

Later, we made up. After a fight, of course. Kinky, or

just the awkwardness of moving into a different relationship? I dunno. I want her, but I don't know how to tell her
what I feel. I don't want to risk saying too much. I wish I
knew what she'd say.

I can't say it first.

I can't bear this. I knew it would happen, after that kiss. Now we have realized that we've got feelings for each other, neither of us knows what to do with them. We're like a bizarre set of traffic lights. Instead of red, red-amber, green, amber, red, we go fight, make up, make love, hide, fight. It's a sequence. We repeat it time after time. We're together – I think. But nobody knows. We're a secret, so we hide our feelings, and we say cruel things to each other in front of the others.

Part of me wants that, because I can't bear the thought of all the comments and jokes and questions there'll be if people find out about us. But part of me wants him to be so proud to have me as a girlfriend that he can't keep it quiet. If he really loved me, he'd want to tell the whole world, wouldn't he?

But he doesn't love me. He's never said it. Me, neither.

SOOZ

We've agreed we fancy each other, that we like sex – yes, it's time to stop the jokes about extra-virgin olive oil and Sooz being vicious because she's frustrated. Sooz has done it, and it was... worth the wait.

So, we carry on with our traffic lights. What we need is peace, privacy, a chance to talk properly without jumping apart every time someone comes through the door. It's driving me nuts.

Maybe I feel a bit more for Jamie than sexual attraction. I think I do. But I can't say it first, can I?

Dear Sooz,

I fancy the pants off you, that's the truth.
I don't want to fight, I want to make... peace.
C'mon, what d'ya say?
If you want to take a chance on your poor
idiot fool who can offer you nothing except a
gorgeous bod and the experience of a lifetime,
I'll see you at my place tonight about 8.
??

J.

Dear poor Idiot Fool,

With an offer like that, who
could refuse?

!!

S.

Suddenly she seemed bigger...

I spent a bit of time getting ready. I looked good, though I say so myself. If I'd been looking into that magic mirror, like the one the wicked queen had in *Snow White*, I would have said. 'Mirror, mirror, on the wall, who is the coolest dude of all?' and it would have breathed, 'You, Stud!'

First Gabi, now Sooz. Women just can't keep their hands off me.

Jamie Collier draws women to him like moths to a flame. What is this irresistible charm, and can we bottle it? Our beautiful reporter Solange DuBois, herself a big fan, gained an exclusive interview with this new phenomenon...

jamie

'Jamie, what are you doing?' Sooz was in the mirror behind me, and the bubble burst.

Sooz. I know all my mates think she's a dog, and I feel ashamed twice over. Ashamed because I'm embarrassed to tell people that me and Sooz are together now, and ashamed because if I love her I know I shouldn't be ashamed of her.

She was kissing the back of my neck. Soft, tender, searching for an answer. And when I kissed her back I could feel the cold steel of the nose ring, the mouth stud, the ripple of gold crusting her ears. But I didn't care. They are part of her, my Sooz. Let them call her freak, android, the bitch from hell. She's mine, and I know what she's really worth.

The kiss progressed. We were on the bed, the temperature was rising. 'Jamie!'

Mum's voice. We froze, like a couple of startled rabbits.

'Rob's here!'

I panicked. Not again! Rob must have a radar for sex hormone, or something. Last time we tried to do it, at Sooz's, he showed up there as well. I had to pretend I'd dropped in to get a CD back.

jamie

Sooz made the first move. I hope she remembers that. She was the one who started scrambling for clothes, not me.

'Jamie!' The door handle rattled. 'The door's locked!'

Sooz was tangled up in a sheet. I got hold of her – she was so small, so soft, so sweet, like an armful of kittens – and I tried to hide her behind my curtains. Suddenly she seemed bigger, harder, all angles. You could tell she was there.

Rob was rattling the door. I wrestled Sooz to the floor and rolled her under the bed. She was completely silent. And out of sight.

Rob only wanted to borrow my CD player. His has gone on the wonk. He must have been gobsmacked when I just handed it over.

'Sure, here you are, mate, I'd love to talk, but... I'm busy getting my coursework together just now.'

Rob looked around the room. No sign of coursework. The computer wasn't even switched on. I could have kicked myself.

'Jamie, mate, are you all right?'

Part of me wanted to tell, honest.

'Yeah, never better. I've got Sooz here actually.

jamie

The ravishing, sexy Sooz is under my bed right now, waiting for you to leave, you sad git, so we can resume our night of passion.'

But how could I? I had no right. It's Sooz's secret, too. She might not have liked to hear his reaction.

'Sooz? You're actually getting it on with Sooz? Wait until everyone hears... Jamie, you're supposed to be such a stud... Sooz!'

All right, I'm not proud of myself. I kept quiet. Finally, Rob left, and Sooz scrambled out from under the bed. There was nothing kittenish about her then. She was the old Sooz, with her armour on and her sword drawn.

She moved towards me, and I took a step back. I know what she's capable of. But for once, she didn't hit me.

'Our cover was nearly blown there for a minute, eh, Jamie?'

The words came out like she wanted to keep it a secret too, but the tone and the body language were, like, how dare you try to hide me. What do you say in a situation like that? I kept quiet, naturally. I knew I was in it up to my neck, but I didn't know why, or how to escape.

'Er, shall we start that again?' I said, with my sexiest James Bond smile.

jamie

Sooz isn't into James Bond.

'Yeah, we'll try again. When you've sorted out whether you really want to, and found a place with a bit of privacy!'

She did hit me then – clever, because I'd decided she wasn't going to, so I wasn't ready. Then the door slammed, and Sooz was gone.

At least she didn't say never again, eh? I have to find somewhere better. I wish I could afford a room in one of those posh hotels.

Never mind, I'll think of something.

jamie

You could hear the smutty smirk on her face.

Have you ever been under the bed while a couple of gay blokes go at it like rabbits above you? No?

There is something about Jamie that attracts disaster. It's like he wears this huge neon sign, only visible to nerds and wankers.

'Want to deal in the improbable? Want to drop shit on someone? Look no further. Step right up. Jamie Collier, magnet for the weird and hopeless.'

Whose idea was it to take over Rob's place for what was supposed to be something more meaningful than a quick shag? Jamie's. Who panicked when he heard someone else arrive, and who didn't have the guts to be caught with Sooz, the bitch from hell? Jamie. Who dived under the bed and trapped us both there while Alex and Mark took full advantage of what they thought was complete privacy? Yes, you guessed it. How did I manage to end up with our generation's answer to Mr Bean? I've spent more time hiding inside cupboards and under beds in the last week than I spent in my entire childhood.

So there we were, under the bed, trying not to listen to the exchange of bodily fluids going on above. (I know some would see it as an educational experience, but I'll spare you the details.) You'd think it couldn't get any worse, wouldn't you? All we had to do was wait until they'd... finished, and then get the hell out of there. And try to act natural when we saw them the next day.

We managed to find a way to pass the time (do you know the world record for a single non-stop snog?). But wait. The satanic forces of fate were a bit bored that day, so they threw in another spanner.

Enter Nicki, whose talent for being in the wrong place at the wrong time will, someday, be legendary. Only Nicki can stumble across a gay love scene and see an opportunity to get flirty.

'Don't get up,' she says, and you could hear the smutty smirk on her face and feel the ripples right through the mattress. Nicki would love to have known where we were just then. She'd have rolled under there with us, and provided us with an expert commentary. She wouldn't have turned a hair. If I didn't hate her so much I might even have admired her for it.

We waited while Al saw Nicki out of the flat, hoping for a chance to escape.

Then Mark answered a call on his mobile. 'On the train, sweetheart, got held up, home soon. Sorry, Rachel.'

Sweetheart, Rachel. Know any blokes called Rachel? Me neither. It would appear our Marky swings both ways.

Unbeknown to your best mate, you are under his bed while he has sex with another man. Immediately afterwards you hear the boyfriend calling his wife.

Do you:

A. Spring out from under the bed, shouting, 'Surprise, surprise, you lying bastard?'

B. Stay hidden, but write an anonymous letter to your mate telling him not to trust his new lurv?

C. Find a hole to crawl into and never, ever, come out?

D. Shrug your shoulders and shag the partner on your left?

No contest for Jamie. Option D. every time.

We met up at his place later, after he had somehow managed to end up in Sasha and Rob's shower, get himself soaked and run down the street in the buff. (Don't ask. I didn't.) He pushed up against me and gave me what was meant to be a smouldering look. It reminded me of those miserable little boxes of matches you get in restaurants. Cheap. And usually damp.

'OK then, Sooz. Time to take up where we left off, eh?'

And he moved in for the kiss. I started to push him off, because the whole thing had grossed me out and I think it's really pervy that he's turned on by it. But his kiss was soft and warm and... suddenly I was ripping the pants off him.

'Jamie, what are we going to do?' We were lounging about in his bed afterwards.

He gave me a horny smile. 'What, you bought a return ticket? Give me a minute, babe, and I'll...'

'About Mark,' I said. 'We've got to tell. Haven't we?'

'We... could. But it might cause a lot of damage, Sooz.'

I considered it. I know people think I'm a bitch, that I don't care about anyone. Just because I'm not a girlie, and I don't simper and drool and wait for a man to come along and protect me. But Al is special. I can't bear knowing that some git is betraying him.

'We've got to tell Al before he gets in too deep,' I said. 'They hardly know each other yet. I know Al will be cut up, but he'll be devastated if it goes on and he falls in love and then finds out. The damage will be much more then.'

'What? No, Sooz, I meant damage to us. If Al finds out we were under the bed, he'll kill us.'

'Jamie! What's more important? Our own stupid skins or the total, utterly total, devastation of our best friend's life?'

'Um...' Jamie thought it was a trick question, and he wanted to please. And my heart sort of swelled up, because he's the only man who's ever wanted to bother trying to find the right answer for me.

I think I might love him. So I hit him as hard as I could.

'Ow! Ow, bloody ow! Ow! What d'ya do that for?'

I grabbed him by the neck. 'Come here,' I said. 'Let Sooz kiss it all better.'

Also available from Channel 4 Books

AS IF nicki's secrets

Gorgeous, bitchy, sexy, selfish – everybody's
got an opinion about Nicki. Here are the
no-holds-barred, private confessions of the
girl who always gets what she wants. And some
might say, never gets what she deserves.